'Extraordinary masterp

– John

'A brilliant writer' – India Knight

'Intense atmosphere and resonant detail . . . make Simenon's
fiction remarkably like life' – Julian Barnes

'A truly wonderful writer . . . marvellously readable – lucid,
simple, absolutely in tune with the world he creates'
– Muriel Spark

'Few writers have ever conveyed with such a sure touch, the
bleakness of human life' – A. N. Wilson

'Compelling, remorseless, brilliant' – John Gray

'A writer of genius, one whose simplicity of language creates
indelible images that the florid stylists of our own day can
only dream of' – *Daily Mail*

'The mysteries of the human personality are revealed in all
their disconcerting complexity' – Anita Brookner

'One of the greatest writers of our time'
– *The Sunday Times*

'I love reading Simenon. He makes me think of Chekhov'
– William Faulkner

'One of the great psychological novelists of this century'
– *Independent*

'The greatest of all, the most genuine novelist we have had
in literature' – André Gide

'Simenon ought to be spoken of in the same breath as
Camus, Beckett and Kafka' – *Independent on Sunday*

GEORGES SIMENON

Maigret Goes to School

Translated by LINDA COVERDALE

PENGUIN BOOKS

PENGUIN CLASSICS

UK | USA | Canada | Ireland | Australia
India | New Zealand | South Africa

Penguin Books is part of the Penguin Random House group of companies
whose addresses can be found at global.penguinrandomhouse.com.

Penguin
Random House
UK

First published in French as *Maigret à l'école* by Presses de la Cité 1954
This translation first published 2017
010

Copyright © Georges Simenon Limited, 1954
Translation copyright © Linda Coverdale, 2017
GEORGES SIMENON ® Simenon.tm
MAIGRET ® Georges Simenon Limited
All rights reserved

The moral rights of the author and translator have been asserted

Typeset in 12.5/15 pt Dante MT Std by Jouve (UK), Milton Keynes
Printed and bound in Great Britain by Clays Ltd, Elcograf S.p.A.

ISBN: 978-0-241-29757-5

www.greenpenguin.co.uk

Contents

1. The Teacher in Purgatory 1

2. The Waitress at the Bon Coin 23

3. Chevassou's Mistress 44

4. The Postmistress's Letters 66

5. Marcel's Lies 86

6. The Postmistress's Funeral 107

7. The Doctor's Forbearance 129

8. Léonie's Horseshoe 148

1. The Teacher in Purgatory

Some images you record unconsciously, with the precision of a camera, and when you find them later in your memory, sometimes you rack your brains to recall where you saw them.

After so many years, Maigret no longer noticed that when he arrived, always slightly winded, at the top of the bare, dusty stairs of the Police Judiciaire, he would pause a moment, glancing automatically at the glassed-in cage that served as a waiting room and was called the aquarium by some colleagues, Purgatory by others. Perhaps they all paused there, in what had become a kind of occupational reflex.

Even on mornings like this one, when clear, bright sunlight as cheerful as lilies-of-the-valley shone on Paris and made the pink chimney pots gleam, a lamp glowed all day in the windowless Purgatory, where daylight entered only from the immense corridor.

Sometimes you'd see some rather disreputable characters in the armchairs and on the green velvet chairs, familiar customers rounded up by an inspector during the night and now waiting to be questioned, or perhaps informers, or witnesses summoned the previous day who looked up with hangdog faces whenever anyone walked by.

I

For some mysterious reason, that was where the photographs of policemen killed in the line of duty were displayed, in two black frames with gold fillets. Other people passed through Purgatory, men and women from what is known as high society, who at first remained standing, as if they'd be summoned any minute now, as if they were there simply for some routine matter. After a good while, you'd see them draw closer to a chair on which they would eventually sit down, and it was not unusual to find them slumped there in dejection three hours later, having lost all sense of their class privilege.

That morning, there was only one man in Purgatory, and Maigret noticed that he was the sort who was commonly called rat-faced. He was on the thin side. His sloped and balding brow was crowned with a froth of reddish hair. His eyes must have been blue or violet, and his nose seemed to thrust itself all the more forwards over a receding chin.

From our schooldays on, we meet people like that everywhere, whom we tend not to take seriously, God knows why.

Maigret felt he had paid so little attention that, if he had been asked, as he pushed open his office door, who was in the waiting room, he might not have known what to reply. It was 8.55. The window was wide open, and a light mist, of a blue tinted with gold, was rising from the Seine. He had put on his between-season overcoat for the first time that year, but the air was still crisp, air you felt like drinking as if it were a light white wine, air that made your face feel taut.

As he took off his hat he looked briefly at the visiting card placed in plain sight on his desk blotter. The ink was pale. *Joseph Gastin, teacher.* Then, in a right-hand corner, in smaller letters obliging him to lean closer, *Saint-André-sur-Mer.*

Making no connection between this card and the rat-faced man, he simply wondered where he'd heard of Saint-André-sur-Mer before. Out in the corridor, the bell rang for the daily briefing. He took off his overcoat, picked up a dossier he had prepared the day before and, as he had done for so many years, set off for the commissioner's office. Along the way he encountered other inspectors, whose eyes all revealed the same mood he'd seen in passers-by in the street.

'This time, spring is here!'

'So it seems.'

'We're going to have a splendid day.'

Sunshine streamed in through the big windows of the commissioner's office as if into a country church, and pigeons cooed on the stone ledge outside.

Everyone who entered rubbed his hands together and said:

'Spring is here.'

They were all over forty-five, and the matters they were about to discuss were of a serious, at times even a macabre nature, yet they delighted like children in the suddenly mild air and especially in the light that bathed the city, turning every street corner, façade, roof and all the cars crossing the Pont Saint-Michel into pictures anyone would be glad to hang on the wall.

3

'Have you seen the deputy director of the bank in Rue de Rivoli, Maigret?'

'I have an appointment with him in half an hour.'

Nothing of importance. His week was practically empty. The deputy director of a bank branch in Rue de Rivoli, a few steps from Les Halles, suspected one of his employees of certain irregularities.

Looking out of a window, Maigret filled his pipe while his colleague from Special Branch discussed a different case involving a senator's daughter who had got herself into a compromising situation.

Back at his office, Maigret found Lucas with his hat already on his head, waiting to accompany him to Rue de Rivoli.

'We're going on foot?'

It was close by. The visiting card had slipped Maigret's mind. Going past Purgatory, he noticed the rat-faced man again, along with two or three other customers, including a nightclub proprietor whom he recognized, who was there in connection with the senator's daughter.

They reached Pont-Neuf, the two of them, Maigret striding along while Lucas, with his short legs, had to struggle to keep up with him. Later on, they would have been hard put to say what they'd talked about. Perhaps they had simply been looking around them. At Rue de Rivoli, the air smelled strongly of fruits and vegetables, and lorries were loading up baskets and slatted crates.

They went into the bank, listened to the explanations of the deputy director, then toured the premises while keeping a discreet eye on the employee under suspicion.

In the absence of evidence, they would set a trap for him. They discussed the details, shook hands. Outside again, Maigret and Lucas found the air so balmy that they carried their overcoats on their arms, which gave them a kind of holiday feeling.

In Place Dauphine, they stopped with the same impulse.

'How about a quick one?'

It was early yet for an aperitif, but they both felt that the taste of Pernod would go marvellously with the springtime atmosphere. They stepped into the Brasserie Dauphine.

'Two Pernods, and quickly!'

'Do you know anything about Saint-André-sur-Mer?'

'I think it's somewhere in Charente.'

That reminded Maigret of the beach at Fouras, in the sun, and the oysters he'd eaten on the terrace of a small bistro at this same hour, around 10.30 in the morning, washed down with a bottle of the local white wine, at the bottom of which had been a little sand.

'Do you think the employee is crooked?'

'The deputy director appears convinced of it.'

'He seems like just some poor fellow.'

'We'll know in two or three days.'

They went along Quai des Orfèvres, up the great staircase, and, once again, Maigret paused. Rat-face was still there, leaning forwards, his long, bony hands clasped in his lap. He looked up at the inspector, who thought he saw reproach in the man's eyes.

In his office, he found the visiting card where he had left it and rang for the office boy.

'He's still there?'

'Since eight this morning. He got here before I did. He insists on speaking to you personally.'

Lots of people, especially the mad and the half-mad, asked to speak personally to the chief of police or to Maigret, whose name they were familiar with thanks to the newspapers. They refused to be seen by any other inspector and some would wait the entire day, return the next morning, stand up hopefully whenever they saw the detective chief inspector pass – only to sit back down and wait some more.

'Show him in.'

Maigret sat, filled a few pipes and motioned to the man now ushered in to take the chair across from him.

'This is you?' he asked, holding the visiting card.

Seeing the man close up, he realized that he had probably not slept, for his complexion was grey, his eyelids red and his eyes glittered unhealthily. The visitor clasped his hands as he had in the waiting room, so tightly that the joints cracked.

Instead of answering the question, he looked at Maigret with both anxiety and resignation, murmuring:

'You've heard the news?'

'About what?'

The man looked surprised, confused, perhaps disappointed.

'I thought everyone knew already. A reporter had arrived before I left Saint-André yesterday evening. I took the night train. I came straight here.'

'Why?'

The fellow seemed intelligent but was clearly very upset, uncertain how to begin his story. Maigret intimidated him. He had probably heard about him for years and, like many people, held him in almost God-like esteem.

At a distance, this had seemed easy. Now he was before a man of flesh and blood puffing gently on his pipe and watching him with wide-open, almost indifferent eyes.

Was this how he had imagined him? Wasn't he beginning to regret coming here?

'They must be thinking that I've run away,' he remarked nervously, with a bitter smile. 'If I were guilty, the way they're sure I am, and if I'd meant to flee, I wouldn't be here, right?'

'It's hard for me to answer that question without more information,' said Maigret softly. 'Of what are you accused?'

'Of killing Léonie Birard.'

'Who is accusing you?'

'The entire village, more or less openly. The lieutenant from the gendarmerie didn't dare arrest me. He admitted frankly to me that he had no proof, but asked me not to go anywhere.'

'You left anyway?'

'Yes.'

'Why?'

The visitor, too tense to remain seated for long, sprang to his feet stammering:

'May I?'

He had no idea what to do with himself or how to behave.

'At times I even wonder what's happening to me.'

He pulled a soiled handkerchief from his pocket and mopped his brow; the handkerchief must have still smelled of the train, and his sweat.

'Have you had any breakfast?'

'No. I was in a hurry to get here. I absolutely did not want to be arrested before that, you understand?'

How could Maigret have understood?

'Why, exactly, did you come to see me?'

'Because I have confidence in you. I know that, if you want to, you will discover the truth.'

'When did this lady . . . what did you say her name was again?'

'Léonie Birard. She used to be our postmistress.'

'When did she die?'

'She was killed on Tuesday morning. The day before yesterday. Shortly after ten in the morning.'

'You are accused of the crime?'

'You were born in the countryside, I read that in a magazine. You spent most of your youth there. So you know how things are in a small village. Saint-André has only 320 inhabitants.'

'One moment. The crime you're talking about was committed in Charente?'

'Yes. About fifteen kilometres north-west of La Rochelle, not far from the Pointe de l'Aiguillon. Do you know it?'

'A little. But I happen to belong to the Police Judiciaire de Paris and have no jurisdiction over Charente.'

'I considered that.'

'In which case . . .'

The man was wearing his best suit, which was shabby; his shirt was worn at the collar. Motionless in the middle of the office, he had bowed his head and was staring at the carpet.

'Of course . . .' he sighed.

'What do you mean?'

'I was wrong. I don't know any more. It just seemed like the right thing to do.'

'What did?'

'To come and place myself under your protection.'

'Under my protection?' repeated Maigret in surprise.

Gastin steeled himself to look up at him, with the air of a man who wonders where he stands.

'Back there, even if they don't arrest me, they might harm or do away with me.'

'They don't like you?'

'No.'

'Why?'

'First, because I'm the teacher and the secretary at the village hall.'

'I don't understand.'

'You've been away from country life for a long time. They've all got money. They're farmers or mussel-farmers. You know the mussel-farms?'

'The ones along the coast?'

'Yes. We're right in the heart of the mussel-farm and oyster-bed region. Everyone owns at least a bit of one. There's big money in it. They're rich. Almost everyone has a car or a small van. Well, do you know how many of them pay taxes on this income?'

'Not too many, I dare say?'

'Not a one! In the village, only the doctor and I pay taxes. Naturally, I'm the one they call a loafer. The way they see it, they're the ones who pay me. When I complain that the children are skipping school, they tell me to mind my own business. And when I insisted that my students greet me properly in the street, they thought I was putting on airs.'

'Tell me about the Léonie Birard case.'

'You'll really listen?'

The look in his eyes brightened with this renewed hope. He forced himself to sit, tried to speak calmly, although his voice still quavered with ill-contained emotion.

'You would have to understand the layout of the village. Here, it's hard to explain. As in almost every village, the school is behind the village hall. That's also where I live, on the other side of the courtyard, and I have a scrap of kitchen garden. The weather on the day before yesterday, Tuesday, was about the same as it is today, a true spring day, and it was a neap tide.'

'Is that important?'

'During neap tides, meaning when the tides are at their weakest, no one goes out to the mussels or the oysters. You understand?'

'Yes.'

'Beyond the school courtyard are gardens and the backs of several houses, including Léonie Birard's.'

'How old was she?'

'Sixty-six. As village hall secretary, I know everyone's exact age.'

'Of course.'

'It's been eight years since she retired. She became almost a complete invalid, no longer leaving her house, where she walked with a cane. A spiteful woman.'

'Spiteful in what way?'

'She hated the whole world.'

'Why?'

'I don't know. She was never married. She had a niece who lived with her for a long time and who married Julien, the tinsmith, who is the village officer as well.'

On another day, these stories might have bored Maigret. That morning, with sunlight bringing a spring warmth through his window, with his pipe that had a fresh taste to it, he listened, smiling vaguely, to the words that reminded him of a different village, where there were also dramas involving the postmistress, the teacher, the village officer.

'The two women no longer see each other, because Léonie didn't want her niece to marry. She doesn't see Doctor Bresselles, either, whom she accuses of trying to poison her with his drugs.'

'He tried to poison her?'

'Of course not! That's to show you what kind of woman she is, or rather, was. Back when she was the postmistress, she used to listen to phone conversations, read postcards, so she knew everyone's secrets. It wasn't hard for her to set people one against the other. Most quarrels among families or neighbours sprang up because of her.'

'So she wasn't well liked.'

'Certainly not.'

'In that case . . .'

Maigret seemed to be saying that, clearly, the death of a universally detested woman simplified things, leaving everyone free to rejoice.

'Except that, they don't like me, either.'

'Because of what you've told me?'

'That and the rest of it. I'm not a local. I was born in Paris, Rue Caulaincourt, in the eighteenth arrondissement, and my wife is from Rue Lamarck.'

'Does your wife live with you in Saint-André?'

'We live together, with our son, who is thirteen.'

'Does he go to your school?'

'There is only one.'

'Do his classmates resent him for being the teacher's son?'

Maigret knew about that as well. He remembered it from his own childhood. The tenant farmers' sons resented him for being the son of the estate manager, who collected their fathers' rent payments.

'I don't show him any favouritism, I swear to you. I even suspect him of intentionally doing less well than he could in school.'

The man had gradually calmed down. You no longer sensed the same fear in his eyes. He was not a madman inventing a story to make himself interesting.

'Léonie Birard had chosen me as her bête noire.'

'For no reason?'

'She'd claim that I egged the children on against her. I state categorically, inspector, that this is not true. On the contrary, I have always tried to make them behave like well-brought-up children. She was very fat, enormous, even. It seems that she wore a wig. And she had a beard: a real moustache and black hairs on her chin. That's enough to stir the children up, you understand? Along with the fact that she would fly into a fury over nothing, like seeing a child's face glued to her window, for example, sticking out his tongue. She would get up from her armchair and shake her cane threateningly. That amused them. It was one of their favourite distractions: going to send old Mother Birard into a rage.'

Hadn't there been, in his village as well, someone like that? In his day, it was the woman who owned the fabric shop, old Mother Tatin, whose cat they all tormented.

'Perhaps I'm boring you with these details, but they have their importance. There were more serious incidents, windows the kids broke at the old woman's house, rubbish they threw inside. She went to complain, I don't know how many times, at the police station in La Rochelle. The lieutenant came to find me, to get the names of the guilty ones.'

'Did you provide them?'

'I told him they were all more or less involved and that, if she stopped playing the scarecrow and brandishing her cane, they would probably lose interest.'

'What happened on Tuesday?'

'Early in the afternoon, at around one thirty, Maria, a Polish cleaning woman with five children, went as she did every day to old lady Birard's. The windows were open, and I could hear her cries from the school, the

13

things she says in Polish every time she becomes upset. Maria, whose full name is Maria Smelker, arrived in the village at sixteen as a hired farm girl and has never married. Her children are from different fathers. People say that at least two belong to the deputy mayor. That one hates me, too, but that's a different story. I'll tell you about that later.'

'So, Tuesday, at around one thirty, Maria called for help?'

'Yes. I didn't leave the classroom because I heard other people rushing to the old woman's house. Shortly afterwards, I saw the doctor's small car go by.'

'Didn't you go and see for yourself?'

'No. There are now some who reproach me for that, claiming that I didn't bother to go over because I already knew what the others had found.'

'I suppose that you could not leave your class?'

'I could have. Sometimes I leave the room for a moment to go and sign papers in the village hall office. I could also have called my wife over.'

'Is she a teacher?'

'She was.'

'In the country?'

'No. We both taught for seven years in Courbevoie, near Paris. It was when I asked to be posted to the countryside that she handed in her resignation.'

'Why did you leave Courbevoie?'

'Because of my wife's health.'

The subject bothered him. He was answering more guardedly.

'So, you did not summon your wife, as you sometimes do, and you remained with your pupils.'

'Yes.'

'What happened next?'

'For more than an hour, there was a huge commotion. The village is usually quite calm. Sounds can easily be heard in the distance. The hammering stopped over at Marchandon's smithy. People were calling to one another over the garden hedges. You know how it goes when something like this happens. I closed our windows to keep the class from getting all excited.'

'From the school windows, can you see into Léonie Birard's house?'

'From one of the windows, yes.'

'What did you see?'

'First, the village officer, which really struck me, because he was not on speaking terms with his wife's aunt. And I saw Théo, the deputy mayor, who must have been half-drunk, as he usually is after ten in the morning. I also caught a glimpse of the doctor, other neighbours, all of them milling around in one room and looking down at the floor. Later, the gendarmerie lieutenant arrived from La Rochelle with two of his men. But I only learned about it when he knocked on the classroom door, and he'd already had time to question a lot of people.'

'Did he accuse you of having killed Léonie Birard?'

Gastin glanced reproachfully at the inspector as if to say, 'You know perfectly well that isn't how such things go.'

And in a slightly flat voice, he explained, 'I saw straight off that he was looking at me in a strange way. The first question he asked me was, "Do you own a rifle, Gastin?"

'I told him that I didn't, but that my son, Jean-Paul, had one. That's another complicated story. You must know how that goes with children. One fine morning, you see someone come to class with marbles and the next day, all the boys are playing marbles, every pocket bulges with them. Another day, someone pulls out a kite, and kites are the new fashion for weeks.

'Well, last autumn, I no longer remember which boy brought out a .22 rifle and began shooting at sparrows. A month later, there were half a dozen rifles like that around. My son wanted one for Christmas. I saw no need to deny him one . . .'

Even the rifle brought back memories for Maigret, except that his rifle, at the time, had been an air-gun, and the pellets had merely ruffled the birds' feathers.

'I told the lieutenant that as far as I knew, the rifle ought to be in Jean-Paul's room. He sent one of his men to make sure. I should have asked my son. I didn't think of it. As it happened, the gun wasn't there: he'd left it in the shed in the kitchen garden, where I keep the wheelbarrow and tools.'

'Léonie Birard was killed with a .22 rifle?'

'That's the most extraordinary thing. And that's not all. The lieutenant then asked me if I had left my classroom that morning, and unfortunately, I said no.'

'Had you left it?'

'For about ten minutes, a little after break time. When someone asks you a question like that, you don't really think about it. Playtime is over at ten o'clock. Then, maybe five minutes later, Piedbœuf, the farmer from Gros-Chêne, arrived to ask me to sign a document he needed to receive his pension, because he's a disabled veteran. I usually have the municipal seal in my classroom. That morning, I didn't have it and I took the farmer to the office. My pupils seemed quiet. Since my wife is not well, I then crossed the courtyard to find out if she needed anything.'

'Is your wife in poor health?'

'It's mostly her nerves. All in all, I was gone for ten or fifteen minutes, more like ten than fifteen.'

'Did you hear anything?'

'I remember that Marchandon was shoeing a horse, because I could hear the hammer blows on the anvil, and the air smelled of burnt horn. The forge is next to the church, almost opposite the school.'

'That's when Léonie Birard was supposedly killed?'

'Yes. Someone, from one of the gardens or windows, seems to have shot at her while she was in her kitchen, which opens on to the back area.'

'It was a .22 bullet that killed her?'

'That's what is most surprising. The bullet wouldn't ordinarily have hurt her much, fired from that distance. Well, it just happened to have entered her left eye and smashed into the inside of her skull.'

'Are you a good shot?'

'People think so, because they saw me shooting targets

this winter with my son. I did that maybe three or four times. Other than that, I've never handled a rifle except at a fair.'

'Didn't the lieutenant believe you?'

'He didn't come right out and accuse me, but he seemed surprised that I hadn't admitted leaving the classroom. Then, while I wasn't there, he questioned the children. He didn't tell me about the results of his interrogation. He went back to La Rochelle. The next day, meaning yesterday, he set himself up in my office at the village hall, with Théo, the deputy mayor, beside him.'

'Where were you meanwhile?'

'I was teaching. Out of thirty-two pupils, only eight showed up. Twice, I was summoned to answer the same questions, and the second time they had me sign my statement. They questioned my wife as well. They asked me how long I had stayed with her. They asked my son about the rifle.'

'But they did not arrest you.'

'They did not arrest me yesterday. I am convinced that they would have today had I remained in Saint-André. At nightfall, stones were thrown at our house. My wife was very upset about it.'

'You left by yourself, leaving her there, your wife, with your son?'

'Yes. I think they won't dare do anything to them. While if I am arrested, they won't give me a chance to defend myself. Once locked up, I won't be able to communicate with the outside any more. No one will believe me. They'll do what they like with me.'

His brow was once again wet with perspiration, and he clasped his fingers together so fiercely that the circulation was cut off.

'Perhaps I was wrong? I thought, if I told you everything, you might agree to come and discover the truth. I am not offering you money. I know that isn't what interests you. I swear to you, inspector, that I did not kill Léonie Birard.'

Maigret reached for the phone, with a hesitant hand, and finally picked up the receiver.

'What is the name of your gendarmerie lieutenant?'

'Daniélou.'

'Hello! Place a call to the gendarmerie in La Rochelle. If Lieutenant Daniélou is not there, see if you can find him at the village hall of Saint-André-sur-Mer. Put him through to me in Lucas' office.'

Maigret hung up, lit a pipe and went over to stand in front of the window. He pretended to pay no more attention to the teacher, who had opened his mouth a few times to thank him but had found nothing to say.

The yellow glint in the air was gradually overtaking the blue, while the façades across the Seine were turning a creamy colour and somewhere the sun was reflecting off the panes of a mansard window.

'Chief, are you the one who asked for Saint-André-sur-Mer?'

'Yes, Lucas. Stay here for a moment.'

Maigret went into the office next door.

'Lieutenant Daniélou? Maigret here, from the Police Judiciaire in Paris. It seems you're looking for someone?'

The officer at the other end of the line could not get over it.

'How did you know that already?'

'We're talking about the teacher?'

'Yes. I was wrong to trust him. I never imagined that he would try to escape. He took the train for Paris yesterday evening and . . .'

'Are you pressing charges against him?'

'Very serious ones. And with the damaging testimony of at least one witness, received this morning.'

'From whom?'

'From one of his pupils.'

'Did he see something?'

'Yes.'

'What?'

'The teacher coming out of his tool shed on Tuesday morning, at around ten twenty. And it was at a quarter past ten that the deputy mayor heard a rifle shot.'

'Have you applied for an arrest warrant from the examining magistrate?'

'I was just about to go to La Rochelle to do that when you called me. How did you hear the news? Have the newspapers . . . ?'

'I haven't read the papers. Joseph Gastin is in my office.'

There was a short silence.

'Ah,' said the lieutenant.

After which he no doubt wanted to ask a question. He did not. Maigret, for his part, was not sure what to say. He had made no decision. If the sunshine hadn't been what it was that morning; if, shortly before, the inspector had not been moved by the memory of Fouras, of oysters and white wine; if Maigret had not been unable to take even three days' holiday during the past ten months; if . . .

'Hello! Are you still on the line?'

'Yes. What do you intend to do with him?'

'Bring him back to you.'

'Personally?'

This was said without enthusiasm, which made the inspector smile.

'Mind you, I would not allow myself to intervene in any way whatsoever in your investigation.'

'You don't believe he's . . .'

'I don't know. Perhaps he is guilty. Perhaps he is not. In any case I am returning him to you.'

'Thank you. I will be at the station.'

Back in his office, Maigret found Lucas observing the teacher in a curious way.

'Give me a moment more. I'll have to clear this upstairs.'

His work would allow him to take a few days off. When he returned, it was to ask Gastin:

'Is there an inn, at Saint-André?'

'The Bon Coin, yes, run by Louis Paumelle. The food is good there, but the rooms don't have running water.'

'You're leaving, chief?'

'Get my wife on the line.'

All this was so unexpected that poor Gastin, thrown completely off balance, did not yet dare to be delighted.

'What did he say to you?'

'He will probably arrest you as soon as we arrive at the station.'

'But . . . you're coming with me? . . .'

Maigret nodded, taking the receiver Lucas held out to him.

'Hello? Will you pack me a small suitcase with some underwear and my toiletries? . . . Yes . . . Yes . . . I don't know . . . Perhaps three or four days . . .'

He added gaily, 'I'm off to the seaside, in Charente. In the heartland of oysters and mussels. In the meantime, I will lunch in the city. See you soon . . .'

He felt as if he were playing a good trick on somebody, like those kids who had pestered old Léonie Birard for so long.

'Come and have a bite with me,' he finally said to the teacher, who rose and followed him as if in a dream.

2. The Waitress at the Bon Coin

The train was in the station at Poitiers when the lamps suddenly lit up all along the platforms, though it was not yet dark. It was only later, while they were crossing some pasture land, that they watched night fall and the windows of the isolated farms begin to shine like stars.

Then, abruptly, a few kilometres from La Rochelle, a light fog came up, not from the countryside but from the sea, and mixed with the darkness. A lighthouse appeared for a moment in the distance.

There were two other people in the compartment, a man and a woman who had spent the whole trip reading, looking up now and then to exchange a few words. Most of the time, Joseph Gastin had kept his tired eyes fixed on the inspector, especially towards the end.

They were going through some switch points. Low houses streamed past. More and more tracks appeared and finally, the station platforms, the doors with their familiar signs, the people waiting, the same people, it almost seemed, as in the previous stations. Hardly was the door opened when they smelled a strong, cool breath from the black hole where the tracks appeared to end and, looking more closely, they made out some ships' masts and funnels, rocking gently, and heard the cries of seagulls, recognized the odours of tar and the tide.

The three uniformed men standing near the exit did not move. Lieutenant Daniélou was still young, with thick eyebrows, a dark little moustache. Only when Maigret and his companion were a few metres away did he step forwards, holding out his hand with military formality.

'It's an honour, detective chief inspector.'

Noticing that one of the sergeants was pulling a pair of handcuffs from his pocket, Maigret murmured to the lieutenant:

'I don't think that's necessary.'

The lieutenant signalled to his subordinate. A few heads, not many, had turned in their direction. People were moving in a herd towards the exit, laden with their suitcases, walking diagonally across the waiting room.

'I have no intention, lieutenant, of interfering with your case in any way. I hope you have understood me. I am not here in any official capacity.'

'I know. The examining magistrate and I have discussed this.'

'He is not displeased, I trust?'

'On the contrary, he's glad to have any help you might bring us. At present, we are obliged to take this man into custody.'

One metre away, pretending not to listen, Joseph Gastin could not help overhearing them.

'In any case, it's in his own interest. He'll be safer in prison than anywhere else. You're not unfamiliar with how people behave in small towns and villages.'

All this was a bit strained. Maigret himself was rather ill at ease.

'Have you had dinner?'

'On the train, yes.'

'Are you planning on staying in La Rochelle tonight?'

'I'm told there's an inn at Saint-André.'

'Will you allow me to invite you for a drink?'

Maigret did not say yes, or no, so the lieutenant went to give instructions to his men, who walked over to the teacher. Having nothing to say to Gastin, the inspector simply looked at him solemnly.

'You heard him,' he seemed to apologize, 'there's no avoiding it. I'll do my best.'

Gastin looked back at him and, a few moments later, turned around for another glance before finally going out the door between the two officers.

'We'd be best off in the station restaurant,' murmured Daniélou. 'Unless you'd prefer to come to my place?'

'Not tonight.'

A few travellers were eating in the poorly lit buffet.

'What will you have?'

'I don't know. A brandy.'

They sat down in a corner, at a table still set for a meal.

'You're not eating anything?' asked the waitress.

They shook their heads. Only after their drinks arrived did the lieutenant ask, in some embarrassment:

'Do you believe he's innocent?'

'I don't know.'

'Before we heard the schoolboy's testimony, we could let him remain at liberty. Unfortunately for Gastin, that testimony is categorical, and the boy seems sincere, has no reason to lie.'

'When did he speak up?'

'This morning, when I questioned the entire class for the second time.'

'He hadn't said anything yesterday?'

'He was scared. You'll see him. If you want, when I go there tomorrow morning, I'll give you the file. I spend most of my time at the village hall.'

There was some lingering awkwardness. The lieutenant appeared intimidated by the inspector's imposing form and reputation.

'You're used to the affairs and people of Paris. I don't know if you're familiar with the atmosphere of our little villages.'

'I was born in a village. And you?'

'Toulouse.'

He managed a smile.

'Would you like me to drive you over there?'

'I think I'll find a taxi.'

'If you prefer. There are some in front of the station.'

They separated at the door of the taxi, which drove off along the harbour road, and Maigret craned his neck to make out the fishing boats in the darkened port.

He was disappointed to have arrived at night. When they turned away from the sea and left La Rochelle, it was to cross countryside that looked like any other, and two villages later the car was already stopping, in front of a lighted window.

'This is it?'

'You asked for the Bon Coin, right?'

A very fat man came to look through the glass door

panel and, without opening it, followed all Maigret's movements as he took out his suitcase, set it down, paid the fare and finally headed towards the inn.

Some men were playing cards off in a corner. The inn smelled of wine and stew, and smoke drifted around the two lamps.

'Do you have a room available?'

Everybody was looking at him. A woman came to observe him from the kitchen door.

'For the night?'

'Maybe for two or three nights.'

He was studied from head to toe.

'Have you got your identity card? The police come by every morning, and we must keep our register in order.'

The four card players were no longer playing, but listening. Maigret held out his card at the counter covered with bottles, and the innkeeper put on his glasses to read it. When he looked up again, he winked slyly.

'You're the famous inspector, hey? I'm Paumelle, Louis Paumelle.'

He turned towards the kitchen to call out:

'Thérèse! Carry the inspector's suitcase to the front room.'

Without paying particular attention to the woman, who must have been about thirty, Maigret had the impression that he had seen her somewhere before, but the thought struck him only afterwards, as with the people he would glimpse when walking past Purgatory. The woman had appeared to give a little start, too.

'What can I get you?'

'Whatever you've got. A brandy, if you like.'

The others, to keep up appearances, had gone back to their game of belote.

'Are you here because of Léonie?'

'Not officially.'

'Is it true that they found the teacher in Paris?'

'He's now in the prison at La Rochelle.'

It was hard to guess what Paumelle thought of this. Innkeeper though he was, he looked more like a peasant on his farm.

'You don't believe it was him?'

'I don't know.'

'I suppose, if you had a mind he was guilty, you wouldn't have gone to this trouble. Am I wrong?'

'Perhaps not.'

'Here's to you! There's a man here who heard the shot. Théo! Isn't that right, you heard the shot?'

One of the card players – sixty-five or perhaps older, unshaven, reddish hair flecked with white, evasive and malicious eyes – turned towards them.

'Why wouldn't I have heard it?'

'It's Inspector Maigret, who's come from Paris to . . .'

'The lieutenant told me about him.'

He did not get up, made no greeting, held his soiled cards in fingers with black nails.

'The deputy mayor,' explained Paumelle quietly.

Maigret replied, equally brief:

'I know.'

'Don't mind him. At this hour . . .'

He tossed back an imaginary drink.

'And you, Ferdinand, what did you see?'

The fellow called Ferdinand had only one arm. His face was that ruddy brown of a man who spends his days in the sun.

'The postman,' explained Louis. 'Ferdinand Cornu. What did you see, Ferdinand?'

'Nothing at all.'

'You saw Théo in his garden.'

'I even brought him a letter.'

'What was he doing?'

'He was planting out onions.'

'At what time?'

'It was exactly ten o'clock at the church. I could see the time on the bell-tower, up over the houses . . . *Belote! Rebelote!* Nine trumps it . . . Ace of spades, king of diamonds, takes the lot . . .'

He slammed his cards down on the table, covered in wet rings from their drinks, and looked defiantly at the other players.

'And to hell with those who come looking to cause us trouble!' he added, getting to his feet. 'You're on the hook, Théo.'

His movements were clumsy, his gait wobbly. He went to claim his postman's cap from a peg and headed for the door, grumbling under his breath.

'Is he like that every evening?'

'Just about.'

Louis Paumelle was going to refill their two glasses when Maigret stayed his hand.

'Not now . . . I assume you won't be closing right away and I've time to go for a walk before bed?'

'I'll wait for you.'

The room was dead silent as he left. Before him lay a public square that was neither square nor round, with the dark mass of the church to the right, while facing him was a shop, its lights out, over which he still managed to discern the words 'Coopérative Charentaise'.

There was a light in the grey stone house on the corner, on the third storey. Walking over to the three front steps, Maigret spied a brass plate, lit a match and read:

Xavier Bresselles
Doctor of Medicine

At a loose end, not sure where to begin, he almost rang, then realized with a shrug that the doctor was probably getting ready for bed.

Most of the houses were dark. He recognized the village hall, a single storey, from its flagpole. It was quite a small building, and in the courtyard, on the second storey of what was probably Gastin's house, a lamp was glowing.

He continued along the road, turned right, passed gardens and house fronts, and in a little while encountered the deputy mayor coming the other way. The man grunted by way of 'Good evening'.

Maigret could not hear the sea, could not see it anywhere. The sleeping village seemed like any other little country town and did not fit the image he had had of oysters and white wine on a terrace overlooking the water.

He was disappointed, for no specific reason. The lieutenant's welcome at the train station had already dampened his enthusiasm. He couldn't hold it against Daniélou. The man knew the area, where he had probably been posted for years. A tragedy had occurred, which he had done his best to resolve, and then Maigret had arrived out of the blue from Paris, apparently convinced that he had things wrong.

The examining magistrate was probably not happy, either. Neither man would dare show it: they would be polite, would let him see their files. But Maigret was still a nuisance, intruding into what was none of his business, and he began to wonder what had made him abruptly decide to make this trip.

He heard steps, voices: probably the other two card players going home. Then, further along, a yellowish dog brushed past his legs, and Maigret jumped, startled.

When he pushed open the door of the Bon Coin, only one lamp was still lit, and the innkeeper, behind his counter, was putting away glasses and bottles. He wore neither waistcoat nor jacket. His dark trousers hung low at his bulging belly, and his rolled-up sleeves revealed fat, hairy arms.

'Found out anything?'

He thought he was clever, probably considered himself the most important person in the village.

'A nightcap?'

'Provided it's on me.'

Ever since that morning Maigret had been longing for some local white wine, but, feeling it no longer suited the late hour, he had another brandy.

'Here's to you!'

'I thought,' murmured the inspector as he wiped his lips, 'that Léonie Birard was not very popular.'

'She was the worst shrew on earth. She's dead. God keep her soul – or, rather, the devil – but she was without any doubt the nastiest woman I've known. And I knew her when she still had plaits down her back and we were in school together. She was . . . hold on . . . three years older than me. Right. I'm sixty-four. So she was sixty-seven. At twelve, she was already a horror.'

'What I don't understand . . .' Maigret began.

'There are lots of things you won't understand, clever though you may be, let me warn you.'

'I don't understand,' continued Maigret, as if talking to himself, 'why, when she was so hated, everyone is hounding the teacher. Because after all, even if he did kill her, you'd think that instead . . .'

'Everyone would say, "Good riddance!" That's what you think, isn't it?'

'Just about.'

'Only you're forgetting that Léonie, well, she was from here.'

He refilled the glasses without being asked.

'It's like in a family, you see. We've the right to hate one another among ourselves and we exercise it often. Let a stranger butt in, and that's a whole different story. We hated Léonie. We hate Gastin and his wife even more.'

'His wife as well?'

'His wife most of all.'

'Why? What did she do?'

'Here, nothing.'

'Why, "here"?'

'In the end people find out everything, even in a back-of-beyond like ours. And we don't like being sent people who aren't wanted any more somewhere else. This isn't the first time the Gastins have been mixed up in a drama.'

It was interesting to watch him, leaning on his counter. He obviously wanted to talk but, with each sentence, he studied Maigret's face to judge the effect produced, ready to backtrack, even contradict himself, like a peasant haggling over a pair of oxen at a fair.

'In short, you arrived without knowing anything?'

'Only that Léonie Birard was killed by a bullet in the left eye.'

'And you came all this way!'

He was making fun of Maigret, in his own way.

'You weren't curious enough to stop off at Courbevoie?'

'Should I have?'

'They'd have told you a fine story. It took some time to make it out here. It was only two years ago that the people of Saint-André heard the news.'

'What news?'

'The Gastin woman was a teacher, along with her husband. They worked in the same school, she on the girls' side, he on the boys'.'

'I know.'

'Have you also heard about Chevassou?'

'Who's Chevassou?'

'A town councillor over there, a handsome fellow, tall and strong, black hair, with a southern accent. There was also a Madame Chevassou. One fine day, when school was letting out, Madame Chevassou shot at Madame Gastin from the street, hit her in the shoulder. Can you guess why? Because she'd found out that her husband and the Gastin woman had been going at it like rabbits. It seems she was acquitted. After which, the Gastins had to leave Courbevoie. They found they had a taste for country life.'

'I don't see the connection to the death of Léonie Birard.'

'Perhaps there isn't any connection.'

'From what you've told me, Joseph Gastin hasn't done anything wrong.'

'He's a cuckold.'

Louis was smiling, delighted with himself.

'There are others, of course. Our village is full of them. Good luck! One last round?'

'No, thanks.'

'Thérèse will show you your room. Tell her what time you'd like your hot water brought up.'

'Thank you. Goodnight.'

'Thérèse!'

She went up the uneven steps of the staircase ahead of him, turned into a corridor with flowered wallpaper, opened a door.

'Would you wake me at around eight o'clock,' he said.

She didn't move, stood there looking at him as if she wanted to confide in him about something. He considered her more carefully.

'I've met you before, haven't I?'

'Do you remember?'

He didn't admit that he recalled only vaguely.

'I'd like you not to talk about it here.'

'You're not from these parts?'

'Yes, I am, but I left at fifteen to work in Paris.'

'Did you really work there?'

'For four years.'

'And after that?'

'Since you saw me there, you know already. Inspector Priollet will tell you that I didn't take the wallet. It was my pal Lucile, and I didn't even know about it.'

An image came to mind, and he realized where he'd seen her. One morning, as he often did, he had walked into the office of his colleague Priollet, superintendent of the Vice Squad. Sitting on a chair was a brunette with dishevelled hair, wiping her eyes and sniffling. There had been something in her pale, sickly face that had appealed to him.

'What did she do?' he had asked Priollet.

'The usual story. A little servant girl who began picking up men on Boulevard Sébastopol. Day before yesterday, a shopkeeper from Béziers complained he'd been robbed and gave us a description that for once was fairly close. Last night we picked her up in a dance hall in Rue de Lappe.'

'It wasn't me!' stammered the girl between two gasping sobs. 'I swear to you, on my mother's life, it's not me who took the wallet.'

The two men had winked at each other.

'What do you think about this, Maigret?'

'She's never been arrested before?'

'Not until now.'

'Where is she from?'

'Somewhere in Charente.'

They often played a little scene of this sort.

'Have you found her friend Lucile?'

'Not yet.'

'Why don't you send this one back to her village?'

Priollet had turned solemnly to the girl.

'Do you want to go home to your village?'

'As long as they don't know about this, back there.'

It was strange to run into her again now, five or six years older, still pale, with big dark eyes that pleaded with the inspector.

'Is Louis Paumelle married?' he asked quietly.

'Widower.'

'You share his bed?'

She nodded.

'Does he know what you were doing in Paris?'

'No. He mustn't find out. He always promises to marry me. He's been promising for years and one of these days he'll make up his mind.'

'Thérèse!' called the innkeeper from the bottom of the stairs.

'I'll be down right away!'

And to Maigret: 'You won't tell him anything?'

He shook his head, with an encouraging smile.

'Don't forget my hot water at eight o'clock.'

It pleased him to have met her again because with her, basically, he was on familiar ground, and it was a little like meeting up with an old acquaintance.

He felt as if he knew the other villagers as well, although he'd hardly seen them at all, because in his village, there had been a deputy mayor who drank, card players (whose game was piquet, for *belote* was not yet in fashion), a postman who thought he was a big man and an innkeeper who knew everyone's secrets.

Their faces remained engraved on his memory. Only, he had seen them with the eyes of a child and now understood that he hadn't known them, not really.

While he was undressing, he heard Paumelle coming upstairs, then bumps in the neighbouring room. Thérèse joined the innkeeper shortly and began to undress in turn. Both were talking in low voices, like a husband and wife going to bed, and the last noise was a creaking of springs.

Maigret had a little trouble arranging his burrow in the two enormous feather mattresses. He rediscovered that country smell of hay and mildew and, perhaps because of the feathers, or the brandies he had drunk in thick glasses with the innkeeper, he was sweating heavily.

Sounds reached him through his slumber before sunrise, including those of a herd of cows going past the front of the inn, mooing now and then. The blacksmith's forge didn't take long to get going. Someone was taking down the shutters below. He opened his eyes, saw a sun yet more glorious than on the day before in Paris, sat up and pulled on his trousers.

His feet bare in his slippers, he went downstairs and found Thérèse in the kitchen, busy making coffee. She was wearing a kind of dressing gown in a floral pattern over her chemise, and her legs were bare. She smelled of bed.

'It isn't eight yet. Only six thirty. Do you want a cup of coffee? It'll be ready in five minutes.'

Neither washed nor shaved, Paumelle descended in turn, in slippers, like the inspector.

'I thought you didn't want to get up before eight.'

They drank their first cup of coffee in thick china bowls, standing, near the stove.

On the square, a few women in black with baskets and two-handled shopping sacks stood in a group.

'What are they waiting for?' asked Maigret.

'The bus. It's market day at La Rochelle.'

They heard hens clucking in the slatted crates.

'Who's teaching at the school now?'

'Yesterday there was no one. This morning, there's a replacement coming from La Rochelle. He should arrive on the bus. He'll stay here, in the back room, since you have the one in the front.'

Maigret was in his room when the bus stopped in the square and he saw a timid-looking young man who must have been the teacher get out, carrying a large Gladstone bag.

The women piled into the bus; the crates were stowed on its roof. Thérèse knocked at the door.

'Your hot water!'

Casually, while looking elsewhere, he asked:

'Are you one of those who think Gastin killed Léonie?'

Before answering, she glanced over at the half-open door.

'I don't know,' she said very softly.

'You don't believe it?'

'It doesn't seem like him. But they all want it to be him, you understand?'

He was starting to understand above all that for no reason he had taken on a difficult, if not impossible, task.

'Who has a stake in the old lady's death?'

'I've no idea. They say she disinherited her niece when the woman got married.'

'To whom will her money go?'

'Perhaps to a charity. She changed her mind so often! . . . Or maybe to Maria, the Polish woman.'

'Is it true that the deputy mayor fathered one or two of her children?'

'Of Maria's? That's what they say. He often goes to see her and sometimes spends the night there.'

'Despite the children?'

'It doesn't bother Maria. Everyone goes there.'

'Paumelle too?'

'He must have, when she was younger. Now she's not very attractive at all.'

'How old is she?'

'Around thirty. She doesn't take any care of herself, and her place, it's worse than a stable.'

'Thérèse!' called the innkeeper, as he had the night before.

It was better not to push it. Paumelle did not seem pleased. Perhaps he was jealous? Or he simply didn't want her to tell the inspector too much.

When Maigret went downstairs, the young teacher was eating and looked at him a little blankly.

'What will you have for breakfast, inspector?'

'Do you have any oysters?'

'Not during a neap tide.'

'Will it last long?'

'Five or six days more.'

Since Paris he had been craving oysters washed down with white wine, and now he was probably not going to get any while he was there.

'There's soup. Or we can make you ham and eggs.'

He ate nothing at all, drank a second cup of coffee, standing in the doorway, looking out at the sunny village square and two silhouettes moving about inside the Coopérative Charentaise.

He was considering indulging in a glass of white wine nonetheless, to erase the taste of the awful coffee, when he heard an eager voice nearby exclaim:

'Inspector Maigret?'

The man was short, thin and lively, with a youthful gaze, although he was past forty. He held out his hand without hesitation and introduced himself.

'Doctor Bresselles! The lieutenant told me yesterday that we were expecting you. I came to offer you any assistance you might need, before I open my surgery. In an hour, the waiting room will be full.'

'Will you have a little something?'

'At my house, if you like, it's next door.'

'I know.'

Maigret followed him into the grey stone house. All the other village houses were lime-washed, some in a raw white, the others in a creamier tone, and the pink roofs gave the place a cheerful air.

'Come in! What would you like to drink?'

'Since I left Paris, I've been wanting oysters and some

local white wine,' admitted Maigret. 'As to the oysters, I've already learned that I'll have to do without them.'

'Armande,' the doctor went to shout at the door. 'Bring up a bottle of white wine. One from the red bin.

'She's my sister,' he explained. 'She has managed my household ever since I became a widower. I have two children, one at the lycée in Niort, the other doing his military service. What do you think of Saint-André?'

Everything seemed to amuse him.

'I forget that you haven't seen much of it yet. Hang on! As a sample, you have that scoundrel Paumelle, who was a farmhand and married the owner of the Bon Coin when her husband died. She was twenty years older than Louis, and partial to bending her elbow. So, since she was fiendishly jealous and the money belonged to her, he did her in sip by sip. Can you imagine? He managed to get her drinking more and more, and it wasn't unusual for her to go back to bed after lunch. She held out for seven years, with a liver like stone, and he was finally able to give her a handsome funeral. Since then, he sleeps with a run of housemaids. They leave one after the other, except for Thérèse, who seems to be hanging on.'

The sister entered, timid, unobtrusive, carrying a tray bearing a bottle and two crystal glasses, and Maigret thought she looked like the servant of a parish priest.

'My sister . . . Inspector Maigret.'

She backed out of the room, and that as well seemed to amuse the doctor.

'Armande never married. Deep down, I am convinced that she has waited all her life for me to become a widower. Now she finally has her house and can spoil me the way she would have spoiled a husband.'

'What do you think of Gastin?'

'A poor sap.'

'Why?'

'Because he does what he can, desperately, and the people who do what they can are poor saps. No one is grateful to him. He labours to teach something to a gang of young snot-noses whom their parents would rather keep on the farm. He even tried to make them wash. I remember the day he sent one home because his head was crawling with lice. Within fifteen minutes the father came running, furious, and they almost came to blows.'

'His wife is ill?'

'To your health! Strictly speaking, she isn't ill, but she isn't healthy, either. You see, I've learned not to believe too much in medicine. The Gastin woman is eating her heart out. She's ashamed. She blames herself every moment of the day for having brought misfortune on her husband.'

'Because of Chevassou?'

'You know about that? Because of Chevassou, yes. She must really have loved him. What's called a devouring passion. You would never believe it to look at her, because she's an ordinary little nothing of a woman, who resembles her husband as sisters do brothers. Perhaps that's the problem, in the end. They are too much alike. As for Chevassou, who's a big brute full of life, a kind of satisfied bull, he did what he wanted with her. She still has some pain in her right arm, which has remained a bit stiff.'

'What were her relations with Léonie Birard?'

'They only saw one another from one window to the other, across the courtyards and gardens, and Léonie stuck out her tongue at her sometimes, as she did at everyone. The most extraordinary thing in this whole business, I find, is that Léonie, who seemed indestructible, was killed by a little bullet from a child's rifle. And that's not all. There are unbelievable coincidences. That left eye, the one injured, was her bad eye, which has always stared a little fixedly and has been blind for years. What do you say to that?'

The doctor raised his glass. The wine had greenish glints, was light and dry, with a pronounced taste of its region.

'To your health! They will all try to trip you up. Don't believe a thing they'll tell you, whether it's parents or children. Come and see me whenever you want, and I will do my very best to help you out.'

'You don't like them?'

The doctor's eyes shone with laughter, and he exclaimed wholeheartedly:

'I adore them. They're priceless!'

3. Chevassou's Mistress

The door to the village hall stood open into a freshly whitewashed hallway along which official notices were tacked up. Certain small ones, like the announcement of a special session of the municipal council, were hand-written, with the headings in Round Hand, probably by the teacher. The floor was of grey flagstones and the panelling grey as well. The door on the left doubtless led to the council room, with its flag and the bust of Marianne, while the door on the right, which stood ajar, led to the secretary's office.

The room was empty, and the air smelled stale with cigar smoke; Lieutenant Daniélou, who for the past two days had made the place his headquarters, had not yet arrived.

Opposite the street door, at the other end of the hallway, a double door stood open on to the courtyard, in the centre of which was a linden. To the right of this courtyard, the low building with three windows visible was the school, with its rows of boys' and girls' faces and the upright figure of the substitute teacher Maigret had seen at the inn.

All that was as quiet as a convent; the only sound was from the hammer on the anvil at the forge. There were hedges and gardens at the back, some tender green beginning to show on the lilac branches, white and yellow houses, a few windows open here and there.

Maigret went to the left, towards the two-storey house of the Gastins. When he reached out to knock on the door, it opened, revealing a kitchen where a boy in glasses, sitting at a table covered with brown oilcloth, was bent over a notebook.

It was Madame Gastin who had opened the door. Through the window she had seen him halt in the courtyard, look around and walk slowly forwards.

'I learned yesterday that you would come,' she said, stepping back to let him pass. 'Come in, inspector. If you knew how much better that made me feel!'

She wiped her wet hands on her apron and turned towards her son, who had not looked up and seemed to be ignoring the visitor.

'Aren't you going to say good morning to Inspector Maigret, Jean-Paul?'

'Good morning.'

'Would you go up to your room?'

The kitchen was small but, even though it was still early morning, perfectly clean and tidy. Young Gastin picked up his book without protest, went out to the corridor and up the stairs.

'Come this way, inspector.'

They went out to the corridor as well and entered the room that served as a parlour, probably never used. There were armchairs with antimacassars of point lace, an upright piano against a wall, a round table of solid oak, photographs on the walls and knick-knacks everywhere.

'Please, do sit down.'

There were four rooms in the house, all equally small, and Maigret felt both too tall and too big there. He had also felt, from the moment he stepped inside the house, that he had suddenly entered an unreal world.

He had been warned that Madame Gastin was a female version of her husband, but he had never imagined her to be so like him that they could indeed be taken for brother and sister. Her hair was of the same nondescript colour, also already thinning, while the middle part of her face seemed thrust forwards, and her pale eyes seemed myopic. As for the child, he was a caricature of both his parents.

Upstairs, was he trying to listen in, or had he returned to his notebook? He was twelve or thirteen and already looked like a little old man or, more precisely, a creature of no particular age.

'I didn't send him to school,' explained Madame Gastin, closing the parlour door. 'I thought it best. You know how cruel children are.'

If Maigret had remained standing, he would almost have filled the room. Sitting quietly in an armchair, he gestured towards the woman to sit down, for it tired him to see her standing there.

She looked as ageless as her son. He knew she was only thirty-four, but he had rarely seen a woman abandon all femininity to such an extent. Beneath her dress of an indefinable colour her body was thin and tired, with the suggestion of two breasts that hung like empty pockets, while her back was beginning to hunch and her skin, instead of colouring in the country sun, had gone grey-ish. Even her voice sounded washed out!

She tried to smile, though, and timidly touched Maigret's forearm as she told him:

'I am so grateful to you for having believed in him!'

He could not tell her that he was certain of nothing yet, or admit that it was the first spring sunshine in Paris and the memory of oysters with white wine that had suddenly impelled him to come.

'If you knew how I reproach myself, inspector! Because I'm the one responsible for what's happening. I am the one who spoiled both his life and my son's. I'm doing my best to atone for it. I try so hard, you see . . .'

He felt uncomfortable, as when you unwittingly enter a house where someone you don't know has died and you don't know what to say. Maigret had just walked into another world, one that did not belong to the village pressing in all around it.

Those three, Gastin, his wife and their son, belonged to such a different race that the inspector understood the country people's distrust.

'I don't know how it will all turn out,' she continued, after a sigh, 'but I don't want to believe that the courts will condemn an innocent person. He is such an extraordinary man! You've met him, but you don't know him. Tell me, how was he, yesterday evening?'

'Fine. Quite calm.'

'Is it true that he was handcuffed at the station?'

'No. He went with the police officers of his own accord.'

'Were there people who saw him?'

'It was all very discreet.'

'Do you think he needs anything? His constitution is delicate. He's never been very strong.'

She wasn't crying. She had probably cried so much in her life that she had run out of tears. Just above her head, to the right of the window, was the photograph of an almost-chubby young woman, and Maigret could not take his eyes off it, wondering if she had ever really been like that, with laughing eyes and even dimples in her cheeks.

'You're looking at my portrait when I was young?'

There was another one, of Gastin, to make a pair. He had hardly changed at all, except that back then he had worn his hair rather long, 'bohemian style' had been the phrase, and he had doubtless written poetry as well.

'Did they tell you?' she murmured, after a glance at the door.

And he felt that this was what she most wanted to talk about, this was what she'd been thinking about ever since hearing that he was coming, this was the only thing, for her, that mattered.

'You mean what happened in Courbevoie?'

'Charles, yes . . .'

She caught herself, blushed, as if this name were taboo.

'Chevassou?'

She nodded.

'I still wonder how that could have happened. I've suffered so, inspector! And I wish someone would explain it to me! You see, I'm not a wicked woman. I met Joseph when I was fifteen and I knew right away that he was the one I would marry. We planned our life together. Together, we decided that we would become teachers.'

'Was he the one who gave you the idea?'

'I think so. He's more intelligent than I am. He is a man of superior gifts. Because he's too modest, people don't always realize this. We earned our diplomas the same year, we got married, and thanks to an influential cousin, we were both sent to Courbevoie.'

'Do you think that this is connected to what happened here on Tuesday?'

She looked at him, startled. He ought not to have interrupted her, because she had lost her train of thought.

'It's all my fault.'

She frowned, anxious to explain herself.

'Without what happened in Courbevoie, we would not have come here. There, people thought highly of Joseph. They have more modern ideas, you understand? He was doing well. He had a future.'

'And you?'

'It was the same for me. He helped me, advised me. Then, one day, it was as if I'd gone crazy. I still wonder what possessed me. I didn't want to. I struggled against it. I swore to myself that I would never do such a thing. Then, when Charles was there . . .'

She blushed again, stammering, as if she were offending Maigret himself by speaking of the man.

'Please excuse me . . . When he was there, I could not resist. I don't think it was love, since I love Joseph and always have. I was seized by a kind of fever and no longer thought of anything else, not even our son, who was quite young. I would have left him, inspector. I really thought about leaving them both, going away, anywhere . . . Do you understand that?'

He did not dare tell her that she had probably never felt sexual pleasure with her husband and that hers was a common story. She needed to believe that her affair was extraordinary, needed to fret, to repent, to call herself the lowest of women.

'Are you a Catholic, Madame Gastin?'

That was another sensitive point.

'I was, like my parents, before I met Joseph. He believes only in science and progress. He hates priests.'

'You stopped practising your faith?'

'Yes.'

'Since that happened, you haven't returned to the Church?'

'I couldn't. I feel it would be betraying him again. Anyway, what would be the point! The first years here, I hoped we would begin a new life. People watched us warily, as always in the countryside. Still, I was convinced that one day they would notice my husband's fine qualities. Then, I don't know how, they found out what happened in Courbevoie, and even the pupils stopped showing him any respect. When I tell you that it's all my fault . . .'

'Did your husband have any arguments with Léonie Birard?'

'On occasion. Because he was the village hall secretary. She was a woman who always stirred up trouble.

There were questions about some benefits that had to be resolved. Joseph is strict. He feels duty bound and won't certify something that isn't true.'

'Did she know what had happened to you?'

'Like everyone else.'

'She stuck her tongue out at you, too?'

'And shouted rude things at me when I walked by her house. I avoided going that way. Not only did she stick out her tongue at me, but sometimes, when she saw me at the window, she turned around and pulled up her skirts. Please excuse me. That an old woman would do that seems almost unbelievable. She was like that. But Joseph would never have thought of killing her for it. He wouldn't have killed anyone. You've seen him. He's a gentle man, who would like the whole world to be happy.'

'Tell me about your son.'

'What do you want me to say? He's like his father. He's a quiet boy, studious, very advanced for his age. If he isn't top of his class, it's because people would accuse my husband of favouring his son. Joseph gives him grades lower than he deserves, on purpose.'

'The boy doesn't rebel?'

'He understands. We've explained to him why we must do it.'

'Does he know about the business in Courbevoie?'

'We've never spoken to him about it. But his classmates wouldn't pass up a chance like that. He pretends not to know anything.'

'Does he ever play with the others?'

'In the beginning, yes. For two years now, since the

village has come out openly against us, he prefers to stay at home. He reads a lot. I'm giving him piano lessons. He already plays quite well for his age.'

The window was closed, and Maigret was beginning to feel stifled, wondering if he hadn't suddenly been trapped in some old photo album.

'Your husband came over here on Tuesday morning shortly after ten?'

'Yes. I think so. They've ask me that question so many times, in every possible way, as if they wanted at all costs to get me to contradict myself, that I'm no longer sure of anything. Usually, during playtime, he comes to the kitchen for a moment and pours himself a cup of coffee. I'm almost always upstairs at that time.'

'He doesn't drink wine?'

'Never. He doesn't smoke, either.'

'On Tuesday, did he come in during playtime?'

'He says no. I said no, too, because he never lies. Then they claimed that he did come in later.'

'You denied this?'

'I was speaking in good faith, Monsieur Maigret. A while later, I remembered having found his empty coffee bowl on the kitchen table. I don't know whether he came in during playtime or afterwards.'

'Could he have gone to the tool shed without you seeing him?'

'The room where I was, upstairs, has no window on the garden side.'

'Could you see Léonie Birard's house?'

'If I had looked, yes.'

'Didn't you hear the shot?'

'I didn't hear anything. The window was closed. I've become very sensitive to the cold. I've always had that tendency. And during playtimes I close the windows, even in the summer, because of the noise.'

'You told me that the people here don't like your husband. I'd like to clarify this point. Is there anyone, in the village, who particularly dislikes your husband?'

'Certainly. The deputy mayor.'

'Théo?'

'Théo Coumart, yes, who lives right behind us. Our gardens are next to each other. Every morning he starts drinking white wine in his storeroom, where he always has a barrel on tap. After ten or eleven, he's at Louis' place and he keeps drinking into the evening.'

'Doesn't he do anything?'

'His parents owned a large farm. Him, he's never worked in his life. One afternoon when Joseph was in La Rochelle with Jean-Paul, last winter, Théo came into the house at around half past four. I was upstairs changing. I heard heavy footsteps on the stairs. It was Théo. He was drunk. He pushed open the bedroom door and started to laugh. Then, right away, as if he were in a brothel, he tried to push me back on to the bed. I clawed him in the face, leaving a long scratch on his nose. It bled. He began cursing, shouting that a woman like me had no right to play hard to get. I opened the window, threatening to call for help. I was in my slip. In the end he went away, mostly, I think, because of the blood running down his face. Since then he has never spoken to me.

'He's the one who controls the village. The mayor, Monsieur Rateau, is a mussel-farmer who has no time to spare from his business and only shows up at the village hall on council days.

'Théo runs the elections as he likes, does favours, always ready to sign any old paper . . .'

'Do you happen to know if he was in his garden on Tuesday morning, as he claims?'

'If he says so, it's probably true, because others must have seen him. Although, if he asked them to lie in his favour, it's true that they wouldn't hesitate to do so.'

'Would it bother you if I had a little chat with your son?'

She rose, resigned, and opened the door.

'Jean-Paul! Will you come down?'

'Why?' said the voice upstairs.

'Inspector Maigret would like a word with you.'

Hesitant footsteps were heard. The boy appeared, a book in hand, staying mistrustfully in the doorway at first.

'Come in, my boy. I assume that you're not afraid of me?'

'I'm not afraid of anyone.'

He spoke in almost the same muffled voice as his mother.

'Were you in school on Tuesday morning?'

Jean-Paul looked at the inspector, then at his mother, as if wondering if he ought to answer even such an innocent question.

'You may speak, Jean-Paul. The inspector is on our side.'

Her look seemed to apologize to Maigret for that affirmation. Even then, the child simply answered with a nod.

'What happened after playtime?'

Still the same silence. Maigret was becoming a monument of patience.

'I assume you want your father to get out of prison and the real culprit to be arrested?'

The thick lenses of the boy's glasses made it hard to judge the look in his eyes. He did not turn away, on the contrary: he stared his questioner full in the face, without a flicker of movement in his thin features.

'For the moment,' continued the inspector, 'I know only what these people say. A small fact, seemingly unimportant, can put me on the track of something. How many pupils are there at school?'

'Answer, Jean-Paul.'

'Thirty-two in all,' he replied grudgingly.

'What do you mean by "in all"?'

'The older and the younger ones. Everyone on the register.'

'There are always absentees,' explained his mother. 'Sometimes, especially in the spring, there are only fifteen or so, and we can't always send gendarmes to see the parents.'

'Do you have any chums?'

'No,' he said curtly.

'There isn't a single one, among the village children, who is your friend?'

At that, seeming to defy the inspector, he announced:

'I'm the teacher's son.'

'Is that why they don't like you?'

He did not reply.

'What do you do during playtime?'

'Nothing.'

'You don't come to see your mother?'

'No.'

'Why?'

'Because my father doesn't want that.'

Madame Gastin explained again.

'He doesn't want to make any distinction between his son and the others. If Jean-Paul came here during the playtimes, there would be no reason why the village officer's son or the butcher's, for example, could not cross the road to go home.'

'I understand. Do you remember what your father did, on Tuesday, during playtime?'

'No.'

'Doesn't he monitor the children?'

'Yes.'

'He stands in the middle of the courtyard?'

'Sometimes.'

'He didn't come to this house?'

'I don't know.'

Maigret had rarely questioned anyone so recalcitrant. If he had had an adult in front of him, he would probably have lost his temper, and, sensing that, Madame Gastin stayed near her son to protect him, placing her hand on his shoulder in a conciliatory gesture.

'Answer the inspector politely, Jean-Paul.'

'I'm not being rude.'

'At ten o'clock, you all returned to the classroom. Did your father go to the blackboard?'

Through the curtains at the window, he saw a section of that blackboard, with words written in chalk, in the building across the way.

'Perhaps.'

'It was a class in what subject?'

'Grammar.'

'Did anyone knock at the door?'

'Perhaps.'

'You're not sure? Didn't you see your father leave?'

'I don't know.'

'Listen to me. When the teacher leaves the class, the pupils usually start getting up, talking, clowning around.'

Jean-Paul kept quiet.

'What happened on Tuesday?'

'I don't remember.'

'You didn't leave the classroom?'

'Why?'

'You might, for example, have gone to the toilet. I see that it is in the courtyard.'

'I didn't go there.'

'Who went over to the windows?'

'I don't know.'

Now Maigret was on his feet, and, in his pockets, his fists were clenched.

'Listen to me . . .'

'I don't know anything. I didn't see anything. I have nothing to tell you.'

Suddenly the boy left the room and went upstairs, where they heard him close a door.

'You mustn't be angry at him, inspector. Put yourself in his place. Yesterday the lieutenant questioned him for an hour, and when my son came home, he didn't say a single word to me but went to lie down on his bed, where he stayed until it was dark, with his eyes wide open.'

'Does he love his father?'

She did not understand the precise point of the question.

'What I mean is: does he have a special affection or admiration for his father? Or else, for example, does he prefer you? Does he confide in you, or in him?'

'He confides in no one. He certainly prefers me to his father.'

'How did he react when they accused your husband?'

'He was just as you've seen him here.'

'He did not cry?'

'I have not seen him cry since he was a baby.'

'How long has he had a rifle?'

'We gave it to him for Christmas.'

'Does he often use it?'

'Now and then he goes for a walk, alone, like a hunter, with the rifle on his arm, but I don't think he fires it often. He tacked a target to the linden in the courtyard a few times, but my husband explained to him that he was wounding the tree.'

'I suppose, if he had left the classroom on Tuesday, while your husband was gone, that his classmates would have noticed?'

'Of course.'

'And they would have mentioned it.'

'You would actually think that Jean-Paul . . . ?'

'I am obliged to think of everything. Which student claims to have seen your husband leaving the tool shed?'

'Marcel Sellier.'

'Whose son is he?'

'His father is the village officer, who is a tinsmith, an electrician and a plumber as well. He also occasionally repairs roofs.'

'How old is Marcel Sellier?'

'The same age as Jean-Paul, give or take a few months.'

'He's a good student?'

'The best, with my son. To avoid seeming to favour Jean-Paul, my husband always gives Marcel the top grade. His father is smart, too, and industrious. I believe that they're good people. Are you very angry with him?'

'With whom?'

'Jean-Paul. He was practically rude to you. And I, I never even offered you anything to drink. Won't you have something?'

'No, thank you. The lieutenant must have arrived, and I promised to see him.'

'Will you keep helping us?'

'Why do you ask me that?'

'Because, if I were you, I think I would be discouraged. You came so far and what you find here is so uninviting . . .'

'I will do my best.'

Sensing that she was about to take his hands in hers,

perhaps to kiss them, he went to the door. He was in a hurry to get outside, to feel the fresh air on his skin, to hear other sounds besides the tired voice of the teacher's wife.

'I'll be back to see you again, no doubt.'

'You don't think he needs anything?'

'If he does, I'll tell you.'

'Shouldn't he be choosing a lawyer?'

'That isn't necessary right now.'

While he was crossing the courtyard without a backwards look, the double glass doors of the school swung open, and a swarm of children rushed outside, yelling. A few of them stopped short when they spotted him, having probably learned from their parents who he was, and watched him pass.

They were of all ages, six-year-old kids and big boys of fourteen or fifteen who already looked almost like adults. There were girls, too, clustered in a corner of the yard as if to get away from the boys.

At the end of the corridor, where the two doors stood open, Maigret caught sight of the local police car. He knocked at the door of the secretary's office.

'Come in!' called Daniélou.

The lieutenant, who had taken off his belt and unbuttoned his tunic, was working at Gastin's desk, with papers spread out before him and municipal stamps all around. He rose to shake hands with Maigret, who did not immediately notice a plump girl sitting off in a dark corner with a baby in her arms.

'Take a seat, detective chief inspector. I'll be with you

in a moment. I've taken the precaution of calling in all the witnesses a second time and going through the inter-rogations again.'

Because of Maigret's arrival in Saint-André, undoubtedly.

'A cigar?'

'No, thank you. I smoke only a pipe.'

'I'd forgotten.'

The lieutenant smoked very black cigars, which he chewed on as he talked.

'If you don't mind,' he said, and turned to the girl.

'You say she promised to leave you everything she had, including the house?'

'Yes. She promised it.'

'Before witnesses?'

The girl did not seem to know what that meant. In fact, she did not seem to know much at all and rather seemed like the village idiot. She was a big, stout girl, solid as a man, wearing a cast-off black dress, and there were wisps of hay in her uncombed hair. She smelled bad. The baby did, too, of urine and poo.

'When was this promise made?'

'A long time ago.'

Her large eyes were of an almost transparent blue, and she frowned in an effort to understand what was wanted of her.

'What do you mean by "a long time"? A year?'

'Maybe a year.'

'Two years?'

'Maybe.'

'How long have you been working for Léonie Birard?'

'Wait . . . After I had my second child . . . No, the third . . .'

'How old is he?'

Her lips were moving, as if she were in church, while she did her mental arithmetic.

'Five.'

'Where is he now?'

'At home.'

'How many are there at home?'

'Three. I've the one here and the oldest is at school.'

'Who's taking care of them?'

'No one.'

The two men exchanged glances.

'So you have been working for Léonie Birard for about five years. Did she promise you right away to leave you her money?'

'No.'

'After two, three years?'

'Yes.'

'Two, or three?'

'I don't know.'

'Did she sign a paper?'

'I don't know.'

'And you don't know either why she made you that promise?'

'To make her niece mad. She told me so.'

'Did her niece use to come to see her?'

'Never.'

'She's Madame Sellier, the village officer's wife, isn't she?'

'Yes.'

'The officer never came to see her either?'

'Yes, he did.'

'They weren't angry with each other?'

'Yes, they were.'

'Why did he come to see her?'

'To threaten to report her for throwing filth out of the window.'

'Did they argue?'

'They screamed insults at each other.'

'Did you feel affection for your employer?'

She looked at him with her round eyes, as if the idea that she could be fond or not of someone had never occurred to her.

'I don't know.'

'Was she nice to you?'

'She gave me leftovers.'

'Of what?'

'Food. And also her old dresses.'

'Did she pay you regularly?'

'Not much.'

'What do you mean by "not much"?'

'Half what the other women pay me when I work for them. But she had me in every afternoon. So . . .'

'Have you seen her arguing with other people?'

'With almost everyone.'

'At her house?'

'She never left home any more; she shouted things out of the window at people.'

'What things?'

'Things that they had done and they didn't want others to know.'

'So everyone hated her?'

'I think so.'

'Did someone hate her in particular, enough to want to kill her?'

'Of course, since someone did.'

'But you haven't the slightest idea who could have done that?'

'I thought you knew.'

'Pardon?'

'Because you arrested the teacher.'

'You think he's the one?'

'I don't know.'

'A question, if I may,' said Maigret quickly, turning to the lieutenant.

'Be my guest.'

'Théo, the deputy mayor: is he the father of one or more of your children?'

She did not seem offended and appeared to be thinking.

'Maybe so. I'm not sure.'

'Did he get along well with Léonie Birard?'

She thought some more.

'Like the others.'

'Did he know that she'd promised to put you in her will?'

'I told him so.'

'How did he react?'

She did not understand the word.

'Well, how did he answer you?'

'He told me to demand a paper from her.'

'Did you do that?'

'Yes.'

'When?'

'A long time ago.'

'She refused?'

'She said that everything was arranged.'

'When you found her dead, what did you do?'

'I shouted.'

'Right away?'

'As soon as I saw the blood. At first I thought she'd fainted.'

'Did you look through the drawers?'

'What drawers?'

Maigret signalled to the lieutenant that he had finished. Daniélou stood up.

'Thank you, Maria. If I need you again, I will send for you.'

'She didn't sign any paper?' asked the girl, standing near the door with her baby.

'We haven't found anything yet.'

Then she grumbled, turning away from them.

'I should have known she was cheating me.'

They saw her pass by the window, looking unhappy and talking to herself.

4. The Postmistress's Letters

The lieutenant sighed, as if in apology.

'You see! I do what I can.'

And it was certainly true. He was even more conscientious now that there was a witness to his investigation, someone from the famous Police Judiciaire and thus particularly impressive in his eyes.

His was a curious story. His family was well known in Toulouse. At the urging of his parents, he had attended the École Polytechnique, and done more than honourably there. Then, instead of choosing between the army and industry, he had opted for the gendarmerie as well as two years of law school.

He had a pretty wife, also of good family, and everyone agreed they formed one of the most charming couples in La Rochelle.

He was making an effort to seem at ease in the greyish setting of the village hall, into which the sunlight was not yet shining and which the brightness outside made look almost dark.

'It isn't easy to find out what they think!' he remarked, lighting a new cigar.

In a corner of the room, six .22 rifles were leaning against the wall, four of them exactly alike and one of an old model, with a carved stock.

'I think I have them all. If there are more somewhere, my men will find them this morning.'

He picked up what resembled a cardboard pillbox from the mantelpiece and took out a deformed bit of lead.

'I've examined it carefully. I once took a course in ballistics, and we have no expert in La Rochelle. It's a lead bullet, what's sometimes called a soft bullet, which flattens when it hits the target, even if it's a pine board. So it's useless to look for the markings found on other bullets, which often allow identification of the weapon used.'

Maigret nodded to show he understood.

'Are you familiar with .22 rifles?' continued the lieutenant.

'More or less.'

More less than more, because he could not remember any crime committed in Paris with such a weapon.

'They can shoot two sorts of cartridges, short or long. The short ones have a weak range but the long ones reach their target at more than 150 metres.'

About twenty other lead lumps formed a small pile on the veined marble mantelpiece.

'Yesterday we did a few experiments with these different rifles. The bullet that struck Léonie Birard is a .22 long, of the same weight as those we fired.'

'The cartridge case hasn't been found?'

'My men went over the gardens behind the house with a fine-tooth comb. They will continue looking this afternoon. It's possible that the shooter picked up the case. What I'm trying to explain to you is that we have very little material evidence.'

'Have all these rifles recently been used?'

'Recently enough. It's hard to judge exactly because the boys don't bother cleaning and oiling them after they're fired. The medical report, which I have here, doesn't help us much either, because the doctor is unable to determine, even approximately, at what distance the gun was fired. It could just as well be fifty metres as more than a hundred.'

Maigret filled his pipe, standing by the window and listening distractedly. Across the way, near the church, he could see a man with bushy black hair shoeing a horse while a younger man held its hoof.

'The examining magistrate and I have considered the various available hypotheses. The first one we thought of, strange as it may seem, is that it was an accident. There's something so unlikely about this crime, there was so little certainty of killing the former postmistress with a .22 calibre bullet, that we wondered if she hadn't been struck by chance. Somewhere in the gardens, someone could have been shooting at sparrows, the way boys do. There have been stranger coincidences. You see what I mean?'

Maigret nodded. The lieutenant had an almost childish desire for his approval and was touching in his eagerness to perform well.

'That's what we called the theory of the pure and simple accident. If Léonie Birard had died at a different time of day, or on a holiday, or elsewhere in the village, we would no doubt have stopped there, because that is the most reasonable theory. Except that when the old woman was killed, the children were in school.'

'All of them?'

'Just about. Three or four who were absent, one of them a girl, live rather far away, on farms, and were not seen in the village that morning. Another, the butcher's son, has been bedridden for almost a month.

'We then thought of a second possibility, that of malice aforethought.

'Someone, no matter which neighbour, feuding with the Birard woman the way almost all of them were, someone whom she had aggravated once too often, could have shot at her from a distance in a fit of rage to frighten her, or break her windows, without even thinking that she might be killed.

'I haven't completely rejected this hypothesis yet because the third one, that of deliberate murder, requires first of all a champion marksman. If the bullet had hit the victim anywhere except in her eye, the wound would not have been too serious. And to hit the eye on purpose, at a certain distance, one would have to be an exceptional shot.

'Don't forget that this happened in broad daylight, in this very block of houses, at an hour when most of the women are at home doing their housework. There's a whole warren of yards and gardens. The weather was fine, and most windows were open.'

'Have you tried to determine where everyone was at around ten fifteen?'

'You heard Maria Smelker. The other depositions are about as clear as hers. People are reluctant to talk. When they go into details, these are so confused that they simply complicate matters.'

'The deputy mayor was in his garden?'

'So it seems. It depends on whether we go by radio time or church time, because the tower clock is fifteen to twenty minutes fast. Someone who was listening to the radio claims to have seen Théo on the road at around ten fifteen, heading for the Bon Coin. At the Bon Coin they affirm that he arrived only after ten thirty. As for the butcher's wife, who was hanging out laundry, she says she saw him go into his wine storeroom for a drink, as he regularly does.'

'Does he own a rifle?'

'No. Only a double-barrelled shotgun for hunting. This shows you just how hard it is to get any valid evidence. The only evidence that holds up is the boy's.'

'The policeman's son?'

'Yes.'

'Why didn't he speak up the first day?'

'I asked him that. His answer is plausible. You're doubtless aware that his father, Julien Sellier, married the old woman's niece?'

'And I know that Léonie Birard had announced her intention to disinherit her.'

'Marcel Sellier thought it would look as if he wanted to put his father out of the running. It was only the following evening that he mentioned it to him. And Julien Sellier brought him to us on Thursday morning. You'll see them. They're nice people, they seem straightforward.'

'Did Marcel see the teacher leave his tool shed?'

'That's what he says. The children in the classroom were left on their own. Most of them were acting up;

Marcel Sellier, who is a calmer, more serious boy, went over to the window and saw Joseph Gastin come out of the shed.'

'He didn't see him go inside?'

'Only leave. At that point, the shot had to have been fired. Yet the teacher continues to deny having gone in the tool shed that morning. Either he's lying, or the boy invented the story. But why?'

'Why indeed?' murmured Maigret lightly.

He felt like having a glass of wine. It seemed about the right time for one. Playtime was over in the courtyard. Two old women were passing with shopping bags, walking towards the cooperative shop.

'Might I take a look at Léonie Birard's house?' he asked.

'I'll go with you. I have the key.'

It, too, was on the mantelpiece. The lieutenant shoved it in his pocket, buttoned his tunic and put on his cap. The air outside did smell of the sea, although still not enough for Maigret. They both headed for the street corner, and in front of Paumelle's place the inspector asked casually:

'Shall we?'

'You think?' replied the lieutenant, a little disconcerted.

He was not the type to drink in a bistro or an inn. The invitation bothered him, and he did not know how to refuse.

'I wonder if that . . .'

'Just a quick glass of white wine.'

Théo was there, sitting in a corner with his long legs stretched out, a half-litre carafe of wine and a glass within reach. The postman, who had an iron hook instead of his left arm, was standing in front of him. Both men fell silent when the other two came inside.

'What can I get you, gentlemen?' asked Louis from behind his counter, his sleeves rolled up high.

'A carafe.'

Daniélou, ill at ease, was trying to act natural. Perhaps that's why the deputy mayor was watching them both with twinkling eyes. He was tall and must once have been fat; when he'd lost weight, his skin had collapsed into folds like a garment now way too big.

His gaze reflected the mocking self-assurance of the peasant as well as that of a politician adept at tampering with municipal elections.

'So, what's happening with that scum of a Gastin?' he asked, as if addressing no one in particular.

And Maigret, without really knowing why, answered in the same tone:

'He's waiting for someone to come and take his place.'

That shocked the lieutenant. As for the postman, his head whipped around.

'You've discovered something?'

'You're the one who knows the area better than anybody,' replied Maigret. 'You cover all your territory every day.'

'And what a day! Before, not too long ago, there were still folks who never got any mail, so to speak. I remember certain farms where I set foot only once a year, for the post-office calendar. Now, not only does everyone receive a newspaper, which must be home-delivered, but there isn't anyone who doesn't receive benefits of some kind. If you knew what that means in the way of forms!'

He repeated, seemingly overwhelmed:

'Forms! Forms!'

To listen to him, you might have thought that he was the one who filled them out.

'First the military veterans. That, I can understand. Then the widows' pensions. Next the welfare payments, the large-family supplements, and the benefits for . . .'

He turned towards the deputy mayor.

'Can you figure it out? I wonder if there's a single person in the entire village who doesn't get something from the government. And I'm sure that some have kids just for the allowances.'

His misted glass of wine in hand, Maigret inquired cheerily:

'Do you think the allowances have something to do with Léonie Birard's death?'

'You never know.'

It was doubtless an obsession. He must have been receiving a pension as well, for his arm. He was paid by the government. And it infuriated him that others also took their turn at the cashier's window. In short, he was jealous.

'Give me a carafe, Louis.'

Théo's eyes were still laughing. Maigret was sipping his wine, and this scene was almost like what he had envisioned for his trip to the seaside. The air was the same colour as the white wine, with the same taste. Two hens were pecking at the hard earth out on the square, where they could hardly be finding any worms. Thérèse, in her kitchen, was peeling onions and occasionally wiping her eyes with the corner of her apron.

'Shall we go?'

Daniélou, who had merely wet his lips in his glass, followed him out in relief.

'Don't you think those peasants seemed to be making fun of us?' he murmured, once outside.

'You don't say!'

'It's as if it amuses you.'

Maigret made no reply. He was beginning to find his footing in the village and no longer regretted having left Quai des Orfèvres. This morning, he had not telephoned his wife as he had promised her he would. He had not even noticed the post office. He would have to get to that soon.

They passed a haberdasher's shop behind the front windows of which the inspector spied a woman so old and withered that it was a miracle she did not break into pieces.

'Who is that?'

'There are two of them, of about the same age, Mesdemoiselles Thévenard.'

Two old spinsters had had a shop in his home village, too. It was as if the villagers of France were interchangeable. Years had passed. The roads had filled with speedy cars. Buses and vans had replaced carts. There were cinemas more or less everywhere. The radio and many other things had been invented. And yet here Maigret was finding once again the characters of his childhood, frozen in their attitudes as if in a naive painting.

'This is the house.'

It was old and the only one in the street that hadn't

been pebble-dashed in years. The lieutenant fitted the big key into the lock of a green-painted door, which he pushed open, and they smelled a sweetish odour, the same that must have reigned in the home of the two old maids next door, an odour found only where elderly people live confined in close quarters.

The first room somewhat resembled the one where Madame Gastin had received him, except that the oaken furniture was less well polished, the armchairs shabbier and there was an enormous set of brass fire-irons. There was also, in a corner, a bed that must have been brought in from another room and which was still unmade.

'The bedrooms are upstairs,' explained the lieutenant. 'During the last few years, Léonie Birard no longer wanted to use the stairs. She lived on the ground floor, sleeping in this room. Nothing has been touched.'

Beyond a half-open door was a rather large kitchen, with a stone fireplace next to which a coal stove had been installed. The whole place was dirty. On the stove, sauce-pans had left reddish circles. The walls were spattered with grease. The leather armchair in front of the win-dow must have been the one where the old woman spent most of her days. Maigret understood why she preferred to stay in this room rather than the one in front: almost no one used the road, which led to the sea, whereas in the back one could view, as from the teacher's place, the liveliest part of the houses, courtyards and gardens, including the schoolyard.

It was almost intimate. From her armchair, Léonie

Birard took part in the daily lives of a dozen households and, if she had good eyes, she could find out what everyone was eating.

'I don't need to tell you that the chalk outline shows the spot where she was found. The stain you see . . .'

'I understand.'

'She hadn't bled much.'

'Where is she now?'

'They took her to the morgue at La Rochelle, for the post-mortem. The funeral will be tomorrow morning.'

'We still don't know who inherits?'

'I've looked everywhere for a will. I telephoned a lawyer in La Rochelle. She had often spoken to him about drawing up a will but had never made one in his presence. He has in his keeping some stocks of hers, some bonds, the title-deeds to this house and to another one she owns two kilometres from here.'

'So that, if nothing is found, her niece will inherit?'

'That is my impression.'

'What does she say about it?'

'She does not seem to be counting on it. The Selliers are not badly off. Without being rich, they have a nice little business. You'll see them. I'm not used to reading people the way you are. I find this family frank, honest and hard-working.'

Maigret had begun opening and closing drawers, discovering half-rusted kitchen utensils, a jumble of objects: old buttons, nails, bills, pell-mell with empty bobbins, stockings, hairpins.

He returned to the first room, where there was an old

chest of drawers that was not without value, and began going through those drawers as well.

'Have you examined these papers?'

The lieutenant reddened slightly, as if he had been caught out or forced to face unpleasant realities.

He'd had the same look in Louis' bistro, when he had had to take the glass of white wine Maigret was handing to him.

'They are letters.'

'So I see.'

'They date back more than ten years, to the time when she was still the postmistress.'

'As far as I can tell, these letters are not addressed to her.'

'That's correct. I will add this correspondence to the file, of course. I've spoken about it to the judge. I cannot do everything at once.'

Every letter was still in its envelope, on which different names were written: Evariste Cornu, Augustin Cornu, Jules Marchandon, Célestin Marchandon, Théodore Coumart, even more, and women's names, too, including those of the two Thévenard sisters, the ladies of the haberdasher's shop.

'If I understand correctly, when she was postmistress, Léonie Birard did not send *all* the mail on to its addressees.'

He glanced at a few letters.

Dear Mama,

This is to tell you that I am well, and that I hope you are the same. I am happy in my new employers' home, except

that the grandfather, who lives with them, coughs all day
long and spits on the floor . . .

Another said:

I met Cousin Jules in the street and he was ashamed when
he saw me. He was completely drunk, and I thought for
a moment that he had not recognized me.

Léonie Birard did not, evidently, open all the letters. She
seemed to pay particular attention to certain families,
especially the Cornus and Rateaus, of whom there were
many in that region.

Several envelopes bore the postmark of the Senate and
were signed by a noted politician who had died two years
earlier.

My dear friend,
I acknowledge receipt of your letter concerning the tem-
pest that ravaged your mussel-farm and carried off more
than two hundred posts. I will see to it that the funds
earmarked for victims of national disasters . . .

'I looked into this,' explained the lieutenant. 'The farms
consist of pine posts driven into the sea bottom and
bound together by bundles of sticks. That's where they
install the clusters of young mussels to fatten them.
When a tide is a little strong, it carries away a certain
number of posts, which are expensive, as they must be
brought from a great distance.'

'So the cunning fellows get them paid for by the government under the guise of a national calamity!'

'The senator was very popular,' observed Daniélou with a wry smile. 'He never had any difficulty getting re-elected.'

'You've read all these letters!'

'I skimmed through them.'

'They provide no clues?'

'They explain why the Birard woman was hated by the entire village. She knew too much about all of them. She must have told them a few home truths. Still, I haven't found anything really serious, nothing bad enough in any case for someone, especially after ten years, to decide to eliminate her with a bullet in the head. Most of the people to whom these letters are addressed are dead, and their children don't care what happened in the past.'

'You're taking these letters away?'

'I don't have to remove them this evening. I can leave you the key to the house. Don't you want to go upstairs?'

Maigret went up, for form's sake. The two rooms, full of strange objects and furniture in poor condition, taught him nothing.

Outside, the lieutenant handed him the key, asking:

'What are you going to do now?'

'What time does school let out?'

'The morning session ends at eleven thirty. Certain pupils, who don't live too far away, go home for lunch. Those from the farms and the seashore bring bread-and-butter with them to eat at the school. Classes resume at one thirty and are over at four.'

Maigret pulled his watch from his pocket. It was ten past eleven.

'Are you staying in the village?'

'I must go and see the examining magistrate, who questioned the teacher this morning, but I'll be back sometime this afternoon.'

'See you later.'

Maigret shook his hand. He wanted another glass of white wine before the classes let out. He stayed there a moment, standing in the sun, watching the lieutenant walk away with a light step, as if relieved of a great burden.

Théo was still at Louis' place. There was also, in the opposite corner, an old man almost in rags, with the look of a tramp, with a bushy white beard. Pouring his drink with a shaking hand, he glanced at Maigret only briefly, without interest.

'A carafe?' asked Louis.

'Of the same as before.'

'That's the only kind I have. I suppose you'll be eating here? Thérèse is cooking a rabbit I know you will enjoy.'

The maid appeared.

'Do you like rabbit in white wine, Monsieur Maigret?'

It was just to see him, to glance at him in complicity and gratitude. He had not betrayed her. She was relieved at that, becoming almost pretty.

'Off to your kitchen.'

A van pulled up; a man entered in the working clothes of a butcher. Unlike most butchers, he was thin and unwell, with a crooked nose and bad teeth.

'A Pernod, Louis.'

He turned towards Théo, who was smiling in delight.

'Hello, you old pirate.'

The deputy mayor simply gestured vaguely with his hand.

'Not too tired? When I think that layabouts like you exist!'

He zeroed in on Maigret.

'So, it's you, it seems, who's going to ferret out the truth.'

'I'm trying!'

'Try hard. If you find out anything, you'll deserve a medal.'

His drooping moustache was getting wet in his glass.

'How's your son?' asked Théo from his corner, his legs still stretched out lazily.

'The doctor claims it's time he was walking. That's easy to say. As soon as we get him upright, he falls down. The doctors don't know anything. No more than deputy mayors!'

Although he seemed to be joking, there was a bitter edge to his voice.

'Done with your day, are you?'

'I still have to do Bourrages.'

He ordered a second glass, drank it down in one go, wiped his moustache and called to Louis:

'Put that on the tab with the rest.'

Then, to the inspector:

'Have fun!'

Finally, he bumped into Théo's legs on purpose as he went out.

'So long, scum!'

They saw him start his van and swing into a U-turn.

'His father and mother died of tuberculosis,' explained Louis. 'His sister is in a sanatorium for TB patients. He has a brother locked up as a madman.'

'And him?'

'He holds his own as best he can, sells his meat in the surrounding countryside. He tried to establish a butcher shop in La Rochelle and lost all the money.'

'Has he children?'

'A son and daughter. The two others died at birth. The son was knocked over by a motorbike a month ago and is still in a cast. The girl, who is seven, must be at school. By the time he's finished his round, he'll have downed a good half-bottle of Pernod.'

'You find that funny?' asked Théo sarcastically.

'Find what funny?'

'To talk about all that.'

'I don't badmouth anyone.'

'You want me to talk about your little doings?'

Looking scared, Louis grabbed a full carafe from under his counter and went to place it on the table.

'You know perfectly well there's nothing to tell. People have to make conversation, don't they?'

Deep down, Théo seemed to be having a ball. His mouth wasn't smiling, but his eyes were glittering strangely. Maigret couldn't help thinking of some sort of old retired faun. There he was, planted in the middle of the village like a malicious god who knew everything that happened inside people's heads and homes, enjoying this show put on for him in solitary pleasure.

He saw Maigret more as an equal than as an enemy.

'You're a very shrewd man,' he seemed to say. 'You pass for a champion at your game. In Paris, you find out everything anyone tries to hide from you.

'Only, I'm a shrewd man, too. And here, I'm the one who knows.

'Try! Play your game. Question people. Worm their secrets out of them.

'We'll see if you ever figure anything out!'

He slept with Maria, who was dirty and unattractive. He had tried to sleep with Madame Gastin, who was no longer any kind of woman. He drank from morning till night without ever getting completely drunk, floating in a world of his own that must have been amusing, because it made him smile.

The old Birard woman knew the village's little secrets as well, but they gnawed at her, working on her like a poison she had to draw out one way or another.

He watched the villagers, scoffed at them, and when someone needed a convenient certificate to obtain one of those allowances that so enraged the postman, he approved it, certifying the document with one of those municipal stamps he always had in the pocket of his droopy trousers.

He didn't take them seriously.

'Another, inspector?'

'Not now.'

Maigret heard children's voices over by the school. The pupils going home for lunch were coming out. He saw a few of them crossing the square.

'I'll be back in half an hour.'

'The rabbit will be ready.'

'Still no oysters?'

'No oysters.'

Hands in his pockets, he headed for the Selliers' shop. A boy had just gone in there before him, winding his way among the buckets, watering cans, sulphate sprayers that cluttered the floor and hung from the ceiling. There were tools everywhere, in a dusty light.

'May I help you?' inquired a woman's voice.

He had to peer into the shadows to find a rather young face, and the bright patch of a blue-checked apron.

'Is your husband here?'

'Out back, in the workshop.'

The boy had gone into the kitchen and was washing his hands at the pump.

'If you'd like to come this way, I'll call him.'

She knew who he was and did not seem frightened. In the kitchen, the vital centre of the house, she brought forwards a straw-bottomed chair for him and opened a door to the courtyard.

'Julien! . . . Someone to see you . . .'

The boy wiped his hands while observing Maigret curiously. And he, too, brought childhood memories back to the inspector. In his class, in all the classes he had been in, there had always been a boy fatter than the rest, with the same frank and studious appearance, and the same clear skin, the same demeanour of a well-brought-up child.

His mother was not big, but his father, who appeared a

moment later, weighed more than a hundred kilos: he was very tall, quite broad, with an almost babyish face and candid eyes.

The man wiped his feet on the doormat before entering. Three places were set at the round table.

'Excuse me,' he murmured, going to take his turn at the pump.

One sensed that there were rituals here, that each person performed certain gestures at certain moments in the day.

'Were you about to sit down to eat?'

It was the woman who answered.

'Not right away. Dinner isn't ready.'

'Actually, what I would most like is a brief chat with your son.'

The father and mother looked at the boy without showing any surprise or uneasiness.

'Did you hear, Marcel?' said the father.

'Yes, Papa.'

'Answer the inspector's questions.'

'Yes, Papa.'

Turned towards Maigret, directly in front of him, he assumed the attitude of a pupil preparing to reply to his teacher.

5. Marcel's Lies

Just as Maigret was lighting his pipe, a kind of silent ceremony took place that, more than everything he had seen since the previous evening in Saint-André, conjured up for the inspector the village of his childhood. For an instant, it was even one of his aunts, also in a blue-checked apron, her hair up in a chignon, who took Madame Sellier's place.

This last had simply looked at her husband, opening her eyes just a little wider, and big Julien had got the message. He went out the door to the courtyard, where he disappeared for a moment. As for his wife, without awaiting his return she had opened the sideboard, taken two glasses from a set, the ones used only for company, and was polishing them with a clean dishtowel.

When the tinsmith returned, he was holding a corked bottle of wine. He did not say anything. Nothing needed to be said. Someone from far away, or from another planet, might have thought that those gestures were part of a religious service. They listened to the sound of the cork coming out of the bottle-neck, the gurgling of the golden wine in the two glasses.

A touch intimidated, Julien picked up one of them and checked its colour, then finally said:

'Cheers.'

'Cheers,' replied Maigret.

After which the man withdrew to a shadowy corner of the room while his wife went over to the stove.

'Tell me, Marcel,' began the inspector, returning to the boy, who had not budged: 'I presume that you have never told a lie?'

If there was any hesitation, it was brief, accompanied by a swift glance in his mother's direction.

'Yes, I have, monsieur . . . But I always confessed it,' he hastened to add.

'You mean you went afterwards to confession?'

'Yes, monsieur.'

'Immediately afterwards?'

'As quickly as possible, because I wouldn't like to die in a state of sin.'

'They mustn't have been important lies though, were they?'

'Important enough.'

'Would you mind much telling me one, as an example?'

'There was the time I tore my trousers climbing a tree. When I came home, I claimed I'd caught them on a nail in Joseph's yard.'

'You went to confession that very day?'

'The day afterwards.'

'And when did you admit the truth to your parents?'

'Only after a week. Another time, I fell into the pond while fishing for frogs. My parents forbid me to play around the pond, because I catch cold easily. My clothes were all wet. I told them I'd been pushed while I was crossing the little bridge over the stream.'

'Did you wait a week again before telling them the truth?'

'Only two days.'

'Do you often lie like that?'

'No, monsieur.'

'Once every how long, about?'

He took the time to reflect, still as if taking an oral exam.

'Not even once a month.'

'Do your friends lie more?'

'Not all of them. Some.'

'Do they go to confession then, like you?'

'I don't know. Probably they do.'

'Are you friends with the teacher's son?'

'No, monsieur.'

'You don't play with him?'

'He doesn't play with anyone.'

'Why?'

'Maybe he doesn't like to play. Or else, because his father is the teacher. I tried to be his friend.'

'Don't you like Monsieur Gastin?'

'He isn't fair.'

'How is he not fair?'

'He always gives me the best grades, even when it's his son who deserves them. I would like to be the best in the class when I've earned it, but not otherwise.'

'Why do you think he does that?'

'I don't know. Maybe because he's afraid.'

'Afraid of what?'

The child tried to find an answer. He certainly sensed what he would have liked to say but realized that it was too complicated, that he wouldn't find the words. He simply repeated:

'I don't know.'

'Do you remember Tuesday morning clearly?'

'Yes, monsieur.'

'What did you do during playtime?'

'I played with the others.'

'What happened shortly after you returned to the classroom?'

'Old man Piedbœuf, from Gros-Chêne, came knocking at the door, and Monsieur Gastin went with him to the village hall after telling us to wait quietly.'

'Does that often happen?'

'Yes, monsieur. Rather often.'

'Do you all wait quietly?'

'Not all of us.'

'Do you, personally, remain quiet?'

'Most of the time.'

'When had that happened before?'

'Also on the day before, Monday, during the funeral. Someone came to get a paper signed.'

'What did you do, Tuesday?'

'At first I stayed in my seat.'

'Did your classmates start misbehaving?'

'Yes, monsieur. Most of them.'

'What were they doing, exactly?'

'They were pretending to fight, for laughs – throwing things at one another's heads, erasers, pencils.'

'After that?'

If he sometimes hesitated before answering, it wasn't

from uneasiness, but like someone trying to find the right words.

'I went to the window.'

'Which window?'

'The one through which you see the courtyards and kitchen gardens. That's always the one I look out of.'

'Why?'

'I don't know. It's the one closest to my bench.'

'It wasn't because you'd just heard a shot that you went to that window?'

'No, monsieur.'

'If there had been a shot outside, you would have heard it?'

'Maybe not. The others were making a lot of noise. And at the forge, they were busy shoeing a horse.'

'Do you have a .22 rifle?'

'Yes, monsieur. I took it to the village hall yesterday like the others did. They asked everyone who has a rifle to take it there.'

'While the teacher was gone, you didn't leave the classroom?'

'No, monsieur.'

Maigret was speaking in a calm, encouraging voice. Madame Sellier had discreetly gone to tidy the shop while her husband, glass in hand, was watching Marcel with satisfaction.

'Did you see the teacher cross the yard?'

'Yes, monsieur.'

'Did you see him go to the tool shed?'

'No, monsieur. He was coming back from it.'

'You saw him coming out of the shed?'

'I saw him shutting the door. Then he crossed the yard, and I whispered to the others, "Watch out!" Everyone returned to their seats. Me, too.'

'Do you play a lot with your classmates?'

'Not a lot, no.'

'You don't like to play?'

'I'm too fat.'

He blushed saying that, and glanced at his father as if in apology.

'Don't you have any friends?'

'Mostly I have Joseph.'

'Who is Joseph?'

'The Rateaus' son.'

'The mayor's son?'

Now Julien Sellier spoke up.

'We have many Rateaus in Saint-André and hereabouts,' he explained, 'almost all of them cousins. Joseph is the son of Marcellin Rateau, the butcher.'

Maigret drank a swallow of wine and relit the pipe he had let go out.

'Was Joseph near you, at the window?'

'He wasn't in school. For a month he's had to stay home because of his accident.'

'He's the boy who was knocked down by a motorbike?'

'Yes, monsieur.'

'You were with him when that happened?'

'Yes, monsieur.'

'Do you go to see him often?'

'Almost every day.'

'Did you go there yesterday?'

'No.'

'The day before?'

'Not then either.'

'Why?'

'Because of what happened. Everyone was busy with the crime.'

'I suppose you would not have dared lie to the police lieutenant?'

'No, sir.'

'Are you pleased that the teacher is in prison?'

'No, sir.'

'Do you realize that he is there because of your statement?'

'I don't know what you mean.'

'If you had not said that you'd seen him leaving the tool shed, he would probably not have been arrested.'

Abashed, the boy said nothing, shifting from one leg to the other, glancing again at his father.

'If you really did see him, you were right to tell the truth.'

'I told the truth.'

'Didn't you like Léonie Birard?'

'No, monsieur.'

'Why not?'

'Because, when I went by, she would shout nasty words at me.'

'At you more than at the others?'

'Yes, monsieur.'

'Do you know why?'

'Because she's angry at Mama for having married my father.'

Maigret half-closed his eyes, looking for another question to ask, found none and decided to empty his glass. He stood up rather heavily, for he had already drunk a fair amount of white wine that morning.

'Thank you, Marcel. If you had something further to tell me, if you were to remember a detail you had forgotten, for example, I would like you to come and see me right away. You're not afraid of me?'

'No, monsieur.'

'Another?' asked the father, reaching for the bottle.

'No, thank you. I don't want to keep you from your lunch any longer. Your son is a smart boy, Monsieur Sellier.'

The tinsmith blushed with pleasure.

'We're raising him the best we can. I don't think he often lies.'

'On that point, when did he speak to you about the teacher going to the shed?'

'Wednesday evening.'

'He said nothing on Tuesday, when the whole village was talking about Léonie Birard's death?'

'No. I think he was intimidated. At dinner, on Wednesday, he seemed different and suddenly he said to me, "Papa, I think I saw something." He told me about it and I went to repeat it to the police lieutenant.'

'Thank you.'

Something was bothering him, he didn't quite know what. Outside, he went first to the Bon Coin, where he saw the substitute teacher eating near the window while reading a book. He remembered that he had intended to call his wife, went on to the post office, which was in a different group of houses, and was served by a young woman of about twenty-five wearing a black smock.

'Will it take a long time to get through to Paris?'

'Not at this hour, Monsieur Maigret.'

While waiting for his call, he watched her doing her accounts and wondered if she were married, if she would get married one day, if she would turn into someone like the old Birard woman.

He spent about five minutes in the booth, and all that the young woman heard through the door was:

'No, no oysters . . . Because there aren't any . . . No . . . The weather is splendid . . . Not chilly at all . . .'

He decided it was lunchtime. The teacher was still at Louis' place, and Maigret found himself sitting at the table opposite his. The entire village already knew who he was. Although they were not greeting him, they followed him with their eyes in the street and, as soon as he had passed, began to talk about him. The teacher looked up from his book three or four times. As he was leaving, he seemed to hesitate. Perhaps he wanted to tell him something? It was unclear. In any case, when he went past, he gave Maigret a nod that could have been taken for an involuntary twitch.

Thérèse was wearing a fresh white apron over her black dress. Louis was eating in the kitchen, where he could sometimes be heard, calling her. When he had finished, he came over to Maigret, his lips still greasy.

'So, what did you think of it, that rabbit?'

'It was excellent.'

'A spot of brandy, to wash it down? On the house.'

He had a protective way of looking at the inspector as if, without him, Maigret would have been lost in the jungle of Saint-André.

'He's quite a character!' he rumbled as he sat down, spreading his knees to accommodate his belly.

'Who?'

'Théo. I don't know anyone shrewder than he is. He's always managed to enjoy life without lifting a finger.'

'So you believe that no one else heard that gunshot?'

'First off, out here in the country nobody pays any attention to a rifle going off. If it had been a shotgun, everyone would have noticed. Besides, those things don't make much noise, and we've got so used to them now that all the kids have them . . .'

'Théo was in his garden and supposedly didn't see a thing?'

'In his garden, or in his wine storeroom, because what he calls gardening is mostly going off to draw a glass from the barrel. Mind you, if he did see something, he probably won't say anything.'

'Even if he saw someone fire the shot?'

'Especially then.'

Pleased with himself, Louis was filling the little glasses.

'I warned you that you wouldn't understand a thing.'

'Do you think that the teacher tried to kill the old woman?'

'And you?'

'No,' said Maigret firmly.

Louis looked at him, smiling as if to say: 'Neither do I.'

But he did not say it. Perhaps they were each feeling as sluggish as the other, after all they had eaten and drunk. They sat for a moment in silence, looking out at the square cut in two by the sun, the greenish windows of the cooperative, the stone portal of the church.

'What's the priest like?' asked Maigret, just to say something.

'He's a priest.'

'Is he on the teacher's side?'

'Against.'

Maigret finally stood up, hesitated for a moment in the centre of the room, then took the lazy way out and headed for the stairs.

'Wake me in an hour,' he told Thérèse.

He should not have been so informal with her. The men of the Police Judiciaire had the habit of treating women like her that way, and it did not escape Louis, who frowned. The green shutters of the room were closed; only thin shafts of sunlight came through. He did not undress, merely took off his jacket and shoes and stretched out on the bedspread.

A little later, when he was just dozing, he thought he heard the rhythmic sound of the sea – was it possible? – then fell completely asleep, waking only at the knock on his door.

'It's been an hour, Monsieur Maigret. Would you like a cup of coffee?'

He still felt heavy, groggy, unsure of exactly what he wanted to do. When he crossed the room downstairs, four men were playing cards, including Théo and Marcellin, the butcher, still in his work clothes.

The inspector continued to sense that some detail was amiss, but could not tell which one. He'd first had that feeling during his questioning of the Sellier boy. At precisely which moment of their conversation?

He began to walk, first towards Léonie Birard's house, the key to which was in his pocket. He went inside, sat down in the front room and read all the letters he had seen there that morning. He found nothing important in them and simply became familiar with certain names: the Dubards, Cornus, Gillets, Rateaus, Boncœurs.

Leaving the house, he intended to follow the road all the way to the sea but a little further along he saw the cemetery and turned in there, where he read on the gravestones more or less the same names he had found in the letters.

He could have pieced together the history of these families, proving that the Rateaus had been allied with the Dubards for two generations and that a Cornu had married a Piedbœuf who died at the age of twenty-six.

As he walked two or three hundred metres further along the road, the sea remained invisible; the meadows sloped gently upwards, while in the distance he saw only a glistening mist, which he gave up trying to reach.

The villagers encountered him in the streets and alleys, his hands in his pockets, stopping sometimes for no reason to look at some façade or passer-by.

Before going to the village hall, he could not resist having a white wine. The four men were still playing cards, and Louis, straddling a chair, was looking on.

The front steps of the village hall were in the sun, and at the end of the corridor, out in the kitchen gardens, he could see the caps of the two policemen. No doubt they were still hunting for the cartridge case?

The windows of the teacher's house were closed. In the classroom, the children's heads were all in rows.

He found the lieutenant annotating in red pencil the official report of an interrogation.

'Come in, sir. I've seen the examining magistrate. He questioned Gastin this morning.'

'How is he?'

'Like a man who has just spent his first night in prison. He was worried that you might already have left.'

'I suppose that he still denies everything?'

'More than ever.'

'Has he a theory of his own?'

'He doesn't believe that anyone tried to kill the postmistress. He thinks it was an act of harassment instead, which proved fatal. People often played mean tricks on her.'

'On Léonie Birard?'

'Yes. Not just the children, the adults as well. You know how it goes when villagers target someone they dislike. Whenever there was a dead cat, it would be tossed into her garden, if not through a window of her house. Two weeks ago, she found her door smeared with excrement. According to the teacher, someone shot at her to scare or infuriate her.'

'And the shed?'

'He continues to claim that he never set foot there on Tuesday.'

'Did he do any gardening on Tuesday morning, before school?'

'Not Tuesday, but Monday. He gets up at six every morning, that's the only time he has a moment to himself. Did you see the Sellier boy? What do you think of him?'

'He answered my questions without any hesitation.'

'Mine, too, without once contradicting himself. I questioned his classmates, who all affirm that he did not leave the classroom after playtime. I assume that, if he were lying, someone would certainly have somehow given him away.'

'I think so too. Do we know who inherits?'

'We still haven't found a will. Madame Sellier seems the likely heir.'

'Have you determined what her husband was doing all Tuesday morning?'

'He was busy in his workshop.'

'Has anyone confirmed that?'

'His wife, first of all. Then the blacksmith, Marchandon, who went to speak to him.'

'At what time?'

'He isn't exactly sure. Before eleven, he says. He claims they chatted for at least fifteen minutes. That doesn't prove a thing, obviously.'

He riffled through his papers.

'All the more so in that young Sellier himself says that the forge was in use at the moment when the teacher left the classroom.'

'So his father might therefore have gone out?'

'Yes, but don't forget that everyone knows him. He would have had to cross the square and go into the gardens. If he had gone by with a rifle, people would have noticed him all the more.'

'But they might not mention it.'

In short, nothing was certain. There was no solid foundation aside from two contradictory statements: the one from Marcel Sellier, who claimed to have seen from the school window the teacher leaving the tool shed, and the other from Gastin, who swore he had never set foot in it that day.

These were recent events. The questioning of the villagers had begun by Tuesday evening and continued throughout Wednesday. Everyone's memories were fresh.

If the teacher had not fired the shot, what reason would he have to lie? And above all, what reason did he have to kill Léonie Birard?

Marcel Sellier had no more reason to invent the story about the shed, either.

Théo, for his part, grumpily stated that he had heard a shot but seen nothing.

Had he been in his kitchen garden? In his wine storeroom? There was no way to rely on the times mentioned by any of them because country people don't pay much attention to the time, unless it's time to eat. Maigret had no confidence either in accounts of this or that person passing by in the street at a particular moment. People used to seeing others ten times a day in the same familiar places no longer pay attention and can, in complete good faith, confuse one encounter with another, or affirm that something took place on Tuesday when it had happened on Monday.

The wine was making him feel hot.

'What time is the funeral?'

'At nine. Everyone will be there. It isn't every day you have the pleasure of burying the village shrew. Have you thought of something?'

Maigret shook his head, drifted around the office, fiddled with the rifles, the cartridges.

'You did tell me that the doctor isn't sure about the time of death?'

'He puts it between ten and eleven that morning.'

'So that, without young Sellier's testimony . . .'

They always came back to that. And each time, Maigret had the same impression that he was narrowly missing the truth, that he had been on the verge, at one point, of discovering it.

Léonie Birard did not interest him. What did he care whether someone had wanted to kill or simply frighten her, or whether it had been an accident that the bullet had entered her left eye?

It was Gastin's situation that fascinated him and, therefore, the Sellier boy's statement as well.

He went to the courtyard and was halfway across when the children were let out of school, emerging less boisterously than at playtime and heading for the exit in small groups. Brothers and sisters could be spotted; some bigger girls were holding smaller kids by the hand, and some children would have to cover more than two kilometres to get home.

Only one boy greeted him, aside from Marcel Sellier, who politely removed his cap. The others went by eyeing him with curiosity.

The teacher was in the doorway. Maigret went over, and the young man stepped aside for him, stammering:

'Do you want to speak to me?'

'Not particularly. Had you already come to Saint-André before?'

'No. This is the first time. I've taught at La Rochelle and Fouras.'

'Do you know Joseph Gastin?'

'No.'

The desks and benches were black, covered with gouges, and violet ink stains made bronze reflections on the varnish. Maigret went to the first window on the left, saw one section of the yard, the gardens, the tool shed. From the window to the right, he could then see the back of the Birard house.

'Did you notice anything today, in the children's attitudes?'

'They're more withdrawn than city children. Perhaps it's from timidity.'

'They weren't huddling together, or passing notes during class?'

The substitute wasn't even twenty-two years old and was visibly intimidated by Maigret, not so much because he was from the police, but because he was famous. The teacher would probably have behaved the same way before a noted politician or a film star.

'I must say that I didn't pay any attention to that. Should I have?'

'What do you think of young Sellier?'

'One moment . . . Which one is he? . . . I don't know all the names yet . . .'

'A boy taller and sturdier than the others, a very good pupil . . .'

The teacher looked at the first seat on the first bench, which was evidently Marcel's place, and Maigret went over to sit there, although unable to slide his legs under the low desk. From that spot, he saw, through the second window, not the kitchen gardens, but the linden in the yard and the Gastins' house.

'He did not seem anxious to you, troubled?'

'No. I remember quizzing him in arithmetic and noting that he was very smart.'

To the right of the Gastins' house could be seen, further along, the second-storey windows of two other houses.

'I might ask you for permission, tomorrow, to come and see the children for a moment during class.'

'I'll be available. We're staying at the same inn, I believe. It will be easier for me if I prepare my lesson plans over here.'

Maigret left him and was about to cross to the teacher's house. It was not Madame Gastin he wanted to see, but Jean-Paul. Halfway there he noticed a curtain moving and stopped, put off by the idea of finding himself once again in a small, stifling room before the unhappy faces of the mother and son.

His courage gave way to a feeling of laziness, absorbed no doubt from the rhythm of village life, the white wine, the sun beginning to vanish behind the roofs.

After all, what was he doing there? A hundred times, in the middle of an investigation, he'd had the same feeling of helplessness or, rather, futility. He would find himself abruptly plunged into the lives of people he had never met before, and his job was to discover their most intimate secrets. This time, as it happened, it wasn't even his job. He was the one who had chosen to come, because a teacher had waited for him for hours in Purgatory at the Police Judiciaire.

The air was taking on a blue tint, becoming cooler, more humid. Windows were lighting up here and there, and Marchandon's forge stood out in red, with dancing flames visible at each puff of the bellows.

In the shop across the way, two women were as still as figures in an advertisement, with only their lips moving slightly. They seemed to be speaking each in turn, and after every sentence, the shopkeeper would nod sadly. Were they talking about Léonie Birard? Probably. And about the funeral the next day, which would be a memorable event in the history of Saint-André.

The men were still playing cards. They doubtless wore away hours like that every afternoon, exchanging the same remarks, reaching occasionally for their glasses and wiping their lips.

He was about to go inside, ask for a carafe and sit in a corner to wait for dinner when a car stopped startlingly close to him.

'Did I scare you?' called the doctor cheerily. 'You haven't ferreted out that truth yet?'

He emerged from the car, lit a cigarette.

'It doesn't look like the Grands Boulevards,' he remarked, waving at the village around them, the dimly lit shop windows, the forge, the half-open church portal emitting a faint gleam. 'You should see it all in the depths of winter. Have you begun to get used to our village routines?'

'Léonie Birard kept letters addressed to different people.'

'She was an old bitch. Some folk called her the louse. If you knew how frightened she was of dying!'

'Was she ill?'

'Deathly ill. Only, she wasn't dying. Like Théo, who ought to have died at least ten years ago and who continues to drink his four daily litres of white wine, not counting the aperitifs.'

'What do you think of the Selliers?'

'They do what they can to join the middle class. Julien arrived here as a welfare ward and has worked hard to make a place for himself. They've only the one son.'

'I know. He's smart.'

'Yes.'

Maigret sensed some reserve in the doctor's voice.

'What do you mean?'

'Nothing. He's a well-brought-up child. He's an altar boy. He's the priest's pet.'

Another one who didn't like priests, apparently.

'Do you think he lied?'

'I didn't say that. I don't believe anything. If you'd been a country doctor for twenty-two years, you'd be like me. All that interests them is to earn money, change it into gold, put the gold into bottles and bury the bottles in their garden. Even when they are ill or hurt, it has to pay.'

'I don't understand.'

'There are always insurance policies, or benefits, some way to turn everything into money.'

He sounded almost like the postman.

'A bunch of crooks!' he concluded, in a tone that seemed to belie his words. 'They're funny. I'm fond of them.'

'Even Léonie Birard?'

'She was a phenomenon.'

'And Germaine Gastin?'

'She'll spend her life torturing herself and the others because she slept with Chevassou. I bet they didn't do it often, perhaps only one time. And just when for once in her life she had enjoyed some pleasure . . . If you're still here tomorrow, come and have lunch with me. This evening I have to go to La Rochelle.'

Night had fallen. Maigret still lingered on the square, emptied his pipe by tapping the bowl against one heel and entered the Bon Coin with a sigh, heading for a table that was already his table while Thérèse, without asking, set a glass and a carafe of white wine at his place.

Across from him, Théo, cards in hand, flashed him a look sparkling with malice, which meant:

'You're getting there! You're getting there! Another few years on that diet and you'll be like the others.'

6. The Postmistress's Funeral

It was not because of the postmistress's funeral, due to take place that day, that Maigret awakened with a weight on his shoulders. The death of Léonie Birard, in broad daylight, had not distressed anyone or offered any dramatic interest, and in the village and on their farms the people of Saint-André must have been dressing for her burial service as gaily as for a wedding. In fact, Louis Paumelle, out in the courtyard early on in a starched white shirt and black cloth trousers – but no collar or tie – was filling an impressive number of carafes with wine, carafes he set not only behind the counter, but on the kitchen table as well, as if for a village fair.

The men were shaving. Everyone would be in black, as though the entire village were in mourning. Maigret remembered one of his aunts, when he was little, whom his father had asked why she'd bought yet another black dress.

'You see, my sister-in-law has breast cancer and might die in a few months or a few weeks. It's so hard on clothes to have them dyed!'

In a village, everyone has so many relatives who can die from one moment to the next that they all spend their lives in mourning clothes.

Maigret was shaving, too.

He saw the morning bus leave almost empty for La

Rochelle, even though it was Saturday. Thérèse had brought him up a cup of coffee and his hot water, because she had seen him spend hours the previous evening off in his corner drinking wine, and then, after dinner, shots of brandy.

It was not because he had been drinking the evening before that he had a feeling of tragedy, either. Perhaps, in the end, the reason was simply that he had slept badly. He had spent the night seeing the faces of children, in close-up, as in a film, faces that resembled the Gastin and Sellier boys but were not exactly either one.

He was trying, without succeeding, to remember those dreams. Someone was angry at him, one of the children, he didn't know which, they were all mixed up together. He kept telling himself that it was easy to recognize them because the teacher's son wore glasses.

Only, immediately afterwards, he saw Marcel Sellier wearing glasses, too, and when he expressed surprise about it, the boy told him:

'I only wear them when I go to confession.'

It was doubtless not so tragic for Gastin to be in prison since the police lieutenant did not believe that much in his guilt, nor did the examining magistrate, either. The teacher was better off over there for a few days, instead of in the village or confined to his house. And one witness report, especially that of a child, would not be enough to condemn him.

To Maigret it was more complicated than that. This often happened to him. It could be said that during each new inquiry his humour followed more or less the same curve.

At the beginning, you see the people from the outside. It is their little troubles that stick out the most and it's amusing. Then, gradually, you get inside their skin, you wonder why they react in this or that way, you catch yourself thinking as they do and it becomes much less funny.

Perhaps, much later, when you've seen so, so much of them that nothing astonishes you any more, it is possible to laugh at them, like Doctor Bresselles.

Maigret was not there yet. The kids preoccupied him. He felt that at least one of them, somewhere, must be living a kind of nightmare in spite of the airy sunshine always bathing the village.

He went downstairs to have breakfast in his corner while carts were already delivering the inhabitants of the most distant farms to the square. The farmers did not come straight to the inn, forming dark groups in the street and in front of the church, and the flash of their shirts looked dazzling against their deep tans.

He did not know who had arranged the funeral, had not thought to ask about that. In any case, the coffin had been brought from La Rochelle and placed directly in the church.

The black shapes multiplied rapidly. Maigret noticed faces he had not seen before. The lieutenant shook his hand.

'Nothing new?'

'Nothing. I saw him yesterday evening in his cell. He still denies the charge, just can't understand why Marcel Sellier insists on accusing him.'

Maigret went to the school courtyard, where there were no classes that day, and the windows of the teacher's house were closed. No one was visible; surely the mother and son would not attend the funeral but stay at home, silent, fearful, expecting trouble.

Yet the crowd did not seem angry. The men called to one another; a few of them began entering Louis' place for a quick one and reappeared, wiping their lips. As the inspector passed, all fell silent, then began to speak in low voices as they followed him with their eyes.

Wearing a tightly belted raincoat even though the sky was clear, a young man came up to him with an outsize pipe in his mouth.

'Albert Raymond, reporter at *La Charente*!' he announced importantly.

He wasn't more than twenty-two, thin, with long hair, his mouth twisted in a sarcastic smile.

Maigret simply nodded.

'I tried to come and see you yesterday, but I didn't have time.'

His words and demeanour made it clear that he considered himself the equal of the inspector. More precisely, that they were both outsiders to the crowd, both able to observe it from on high, as people in the know, who have explored every last little corner of human nature.

'Is it true,' he asked, pad and pencil in hand, 'that the teacher went to offer you his savings so that you would get him out of trouble?'

Maigret turned to him, looked him up and down, was about to open his mouth and then, with a shrug, turned his back on him.

The fool was probably going to imagine that he had

struck home. It was of no importance. Bells were ringing. The women filled the entire church, along with a few men. There was a murmuring of organ music, the altar boy's bell.

'Will there be a mass, or only an absolution?' the inspector asked someone he did not know.

'A mass and an absolution. We have enough time.'

Enough time to go and have a drink at Louis' place. Most of the men had gradually gathered in front of the inn, going inside in groups, standing around and downing a carafe or two, then coming back outside. There was constant coming and going, with men in the kitchen and even in the courtyard. Louis Paumelle, who had found time to go inside the church, had removed his jacket and was hard at work, helped by Thérèse and a young man who seemed accustomed to lending him a hand.

Sellier and his wife were attending the service. Maigret had not seen their son Marcel but saw why a little later, when he entered the church in turn. Marcel was there, in the surplice of an altar boy, assisting at the mass. He must have been able to go directly to the sacristy, cutting through his parents' courtyard.

'*Dies irae, dies illa . . .*'

The women were moving their lips and actually seemed as if they were praying. Was it for the soul of Léonie Birard that they prayed, or for themselves? A few old men were at the back of the nave, hats in hand, and others came now and then to peek through the door to see how far along the service was.

Maigret came back outside and noticed Théo, who, by

way of a greeting, gave him his usual smile dripping with irony.

Someone certainly knew. Perhaps even several did and were keeping quiet? Inside the Bon Coin, voices were growing louder, and a lean farmer with a drooping moustache was already more than half-drunk.

The butcher as well, Maigret suspected, was walking less steadily, his eyes unusually bright, and Maigret saw him empty three big glasses with one man or another in the space of a few minutes.

Less intrigued than the inspector, or more put off by the crowd's inquisitiveness, the lieutenant was keeping to the secretariat of the village hall, where the courtyard was empty around the linden.

A cart passed, serving as a hearse and pulled by a chestnut horse with a black cloth over its back. The cart pulled up in front of the church, and the driver came over for a drink.

There was a light breeze stirring. A few clouds, way up in the sky, gleamed like mother-of-pearl.

Finally the church doors opened. The drinkers rushed over. The coffin emerged borne by four men, among whom Maigret recognized Julien Sellier and the deputy mayor.

They hoisted it up on to the cart, not without difficulty. They covered it with a black cloth with a silver fringe. Then young Sellier appeared, carrying the silver cross at the end of a staff of black wood, and his surplice puffed up two or three times like a balloon.

The priest followed, reciting prayers, finding the time

to observe each person around him and to stare for an instant at Maigret.

Next came Julien Sellier and his wife, both in black, she with a crêpe veil over her face. The mayor followed, a tall, strong man, composed, grey-haired, with an entourage of municipal councillors, and then came the bulk of the crowd, the men first, the women after them and some – especially at the end of the cortège – dragging a child along by the hand.

The young reporter came and went, taking notes, talking to people whom Maigret did not know. Advancing slowly, the cortège passed the Bon Coin, where Thérèse stood alone in the doorway, as Paumelle had joined the group of councillors.

For the second time that morning Maigret was tempted to go and knock on the Gastins' door and talk to Jean-Paul. While all the others were going to the cemetery, weren't the mother and son feeling more alone than ever in the deserted village?

He followed the rest, for no particular reason. They passed Léonie Birard's house, then a farm where a calf in the yard began to bawl.

At the entrance to the cemetery there was some milling about, slightly disorganized. The priest and altar boy were already at the grave before everyone had entered the burial ground.

That was when Maigret spotted a face looking over the wall. He recognized Jean-Paul. One of the lenses in his glasses was reflecting the sun like a mirror.

Instead of following the crowd, the inspector hung

back and began walking around the cemetery, intending to reach Jean-Paul. Wouldn't the boy be too intent on what was happening around the grave to notice his manoeuvre?

He was walking through a stretch of waste ground. When he was only about thirty metres from the child, he stepped on a dead branch.

Jean-Paul instantly looked over in his direction, jumped off the stone he'd been standing on and dashed towards the road.

Maigret almost called after him, but the others would have heard him, so he simply quickened his pace, hoping to catch up with the boy along the way.

It was a ridiculous situation, he realized that. He didn't dare run. Neither did Jean-Paul. The child was even too scared to look back. He was in school clothes, doubtless the only one in the village not wearing his Sunday best.

The boy probably wanted to go home and thus ought to have passed by the gate to the cemetery, where there was a group of farmers.

He turned left, towards the sea, perhaps hoping that the inspector would not follow him.

Maigret followed him. There were no more farms or houses, only fields and some meadows where a few cows were grazing. A hillock was still hiding the sea. The road was climbing slightly.

The boy walked as fast as he could without running, and Maigret, at his end, lengthened his stride. He did not even know exactly why he was pursuing the child like this and quickly realized that it was cruel.

To Jean-Paul, he must have represented a formidable power hot on his heels. But the inspector could hardly start shouting:

'Jean-Paul! . . . Stop! . . . I simply want to talk to you . . . !'

The cemetery had disappeared behind them, along with the village. Cresting the hillock, the Gastin boy began going down the other side; Maigret saw only his upper body, then his head. An instant later, he saw nothing, until he reached the hilltop himself and then, at last, he discovered the shimmering expanse of the sea, with what looked to him like an island in the distance, or else the Pointe de l'Aiguillon, and a few fishing boats with brown sails seemingly suspended in space.

Jean-Paul was still walking. There was no path to the left or right. At the shore stood five or six red-roofed shacks where the mussel-farmers stored their equipment.

Maigret made up his mind.

'Jean-Paul!'

His voice sounded so strange that he barely recognized it and turned around to make sure no one was watching him. He noticed a brief hitch in the child's pace; surprise at his call had almost halted the boy in hesitation, but he was again walking as fast as ever, almost running, now in a panic.

Feeling like a big brute tormenting a defenceless creature, the inspector was ashamed when he called out again.

'Hey, kid, stop . . .'

The most ridiculous part was that he was out of breath, and his voice was not carrying. He and the boy were still about the same distance apart. To get closer, he would have had to run.

What was Jean-Paul hoping for? That Maigret would become discouraged and turn back?

It was more plausible that he wasn't thinking at all, that he was hurrying straight ahead as if this were the sole way to escape from danger. At the end of the road there was only the sea, with its shining fringe rolling across the shingle beach.

'Jean-Paul . . .'

At this point, it would have been just as stupid to give up as to go on.

The boy reached the shore, paused before following the path that must have led to the next village and halted at last, with his back to Maigret. Only when he heard the inspector's footsteps coming quite close did he turn to face him.

He was not red, but pale, with pinched nostrils. He was clearly panting rapidly, lips parted, and you felt you could hear his heart beating like that of a bird held in your hand.

Maigret said nothing. He could not find anything to say just then and he, too, needed to catch his breath.

Jean-Paul, no longer looking at him, had turned towards the sea. They both stared at it, and the silence lasted for a long time, as long as it took for their hearts to calm down to a steady pulse.

Then Maigret walked a few steps to sit down on a pile of posts that smelled of fresh pine. He took off his hat, mopped his brow unashamedly and, very slowly, filled a pipe.

'You walk fast,' he finally murmured.

The boy, standing stiff-legged like a young rooster, did not reply.

'Won't you come over and sit near me?'

'I don't feel like sitting down.'

'Are you angry?'

With a brief glance at him, Jean-Paul asked:

'Why?'

'I wanted to talk to you without your mother around. At your house, it's impossible. When I spotted you over the cemetery wall, I thought it might be a good opportunity.'

He left long silences between his sentences, to avoid spooking the boy.

'What were you looking at?'

'The people.'

'You couldn't look at everyone all at once. I'm sure you were looking at someone in particular. Am I right?'

Jean-Paul did not say yes, or deny anything, either.

'Do you usually go to church?'

'No.'

'Why not?'

'Because my parents don't go.'

With an adult, this would have been easier. It had been a long time since Maigret was a child. He had neither son nor daughter, yet he had to try to think like this boy.

'Did you tell your mother you were going out this morning?'

'No.'

'You didn't want her to know?'

'She would have stopped me.'

'You took advantage of her being upstairs to slip out quietly? And you made your way along the alleys?'

'I wanted to see.'

'What?'

It wasn't the crowd, or the coffin being lowered into the grave. Maigret would have sworn to that.

He remembered the surplice billowing in the breeze, the cross Marcel carried, recalled the time when he was barely seven and had wanted so much to be an altar boy. He'd had to wait two years. He, too, had carried the silver cross, trotting in front of a country hearse towards the cemetery.

'You wanted to see Marcel?'

He saw him give a start, with a child's astonishment at abruptly learning that a grown-up can read his mind.

'Why aren't you friends with Marcel?'

'I'm not friends with anybody.'

'You don't like anybody?'

'I'm the teacher's son, I already told you.'

'You'd rather be the son of the tinsmith, or the mayor, or any farmer at all from the village?'

'I didn't say that.'

He had to be careful not to frighten him, which might well have set him off again at a run. And yet it wasn't simply the fear of Maigret catching him again that was keeping the boy there. He was faster than the inspector. Now that they were face to face, did he not feel a kind of relief? And, deep in his heart, a secret longing to talk to someone?

'You still don't want to sit down?'

'I'd rather keep standing.'

'Are you sorry that your father is in prison?'

Instead of replying 'No' right away, he remained silent.

'You aren't sad about that?'

And Maigret felt as if he were stalking his objective, advancing only with infinite caution. He mustn't move too quickly. Even a single word could so threaten the child that he would reveal nothing further.

'Does it hurt you not to be like the others?'

'Why am I not like them? Who told you that?'

'Suppose I have a son, who goes to school, plays in the neighbourhood streets. His classmates would say, "He's the inspector's son!"'

'And because of that, they wouldn't treat him exactly like the other children. You see?'

'You, you're the teacher's son.'

The youngster shot him a longer look this time, more penetrating than before.

'Would you have liked to be an altar boy?'

He could tell he was on the wrong track. It was hard to say how he knew. Certain words provoked barely perceptible reactions. With others, it was as if Jean-Paul were closing up.

'Does Marcel have friends?'

'Yes.'

'When they're together, do they talk quietly? Exchange secrets, start laughing while they're looking at the rest of the kids?'

That had come back to him from so long ago that it surprised him. It was the first time, he felt, that he was encountering such vivid memories of his own childhood, to the point of smelling the scent of the schoolyard back then, when the lilacs were in bloom.

'Did you try to be their friend?'

'No.'

'Why not?'

'No reason.'

'You thought they wouldn't go along?'

'Why are you asking me these questions?'

'Because your father is in prison. He did not shoot at Léonie Birard.'

He was studying the youngster's eyes, and the boy did not flinch.

'You know perfectly well he didn't. Therefore, someone else did. Would you like your father to be convicted?'

'No.'

There had been a barely perceptible hesitation, and Maigret decided not to press the point. He had already considered that idea, in his corner the previous evening, wondering if, deep in his heart, Jean-Paul might be angry at his father and mother for not being like the other parents.

Not only because his father was a teacher. They did not go to church. They did not dress him like the other children. Their house was not like the other houses, either, and their life was different. His mother never laughed but slipped around like a shadow, humble and repentant. She had done something very bad, and a woman had shot at her, to punish her.

That woman had not been convicted, which proved

that she was right. Perhaps Jean-Paul loved them anyway? Whether he liked it or not, he belonged to the clan, was of their kind.

All that was difficult to express. There were nuances that disappeared when things were put into words.

'Suppose you know something that's enough to get your father out of prison . . .'

With no idea himself where he was going, Maigret was surprised to see Jean-Paul look up abruptly to stare at him in a mixture of fright and admiration. The boy opened his mouth, almost spoke, but didn't, clenching his fists in the effort to control himself.

'You see, I'm only trying to understand. I don't know your father well, but I am convinced that he's a man who does not lie. He says that he did not set foot inside the tool shed on Tuesday morning, and I believe him.'

Jean-Paul, still on the defensive, kept watching the inspector.

'On the other hand, Marcel Sellier seems like a good boy. When he does happen to lie, he goes right away to confession so as not to remain in a state of sin. He has no reason to accuse your father, who, instead of being unfair to him, always grades him at the head of the class, when you should be there.

'Well, Marcel claims he saw your father coming out of the tool shed.'

It was like a bubble rising suddenly to the surface of a pond. His head hanging, Jean-Paul said firmly, without looking at Maigret:

'He's lying.'

'You're sure he's lying, right? It isn't some vague feeling. And you aren't saying it from jealousy, either.'

'I'm not jealous of him.'

'Why didn't you say this sooner?'

'What?'

'That Marcel was lying.'

'Because!'

'You're certain that he did not see your father?'

'Yes.'

'How come?'

Maigret had expected tears, perhaps shouting, but Jean-Paul's eyes were dry behind his glasses. Except that his body had relaxed. There was no longer anything aggressive in his attitude. He was not even on the defensive any more.

The only sign of his surrender was that, feeling wobbly on his feet, he sat down a short distance from the inspector.

'I saw him.'

'Whom did you see?'

'Marcel.'

'Where? When?'

'In the classroom, near the window.'

'Tell me precisely what happened.'

'Nothing happened. Monsieur Piedbœuf came to get my father. They both went off towards the village hall office.'

'You saw them?'

'Yes. I could see them from my seat. They disappeared through the arch at the entrance, and all the pupils began to fool around, as usual.'

'You did not leave your bench?'

'No.'

'You never misbehave?'

'I don't.'

'Where was Marcel?'

'Near the first window on the left, the one that over-looks the schoolyard and the gardens.'

'What was he doing?'

'Nothing. He was looking outside.'

'He doesn't misbehave either?'

'Not often.'

'Sometimes?'

'When Joseph is there.'

'The butcher's son?'

'Yes.'

'You were sitting at your desk. Marcel was near the left-hand window. Your father and Monsieur Piedbœuf were in the office. That is correct?'

'Yes.'

'The windows were open?'

'They were closed.'

'You could still hear the noise from the forge?'

'I think so. I'm almost certain.'

'What happened?'

'Marcel left the window and crossed the classroom.'

'To go where?'

'To one of the two windows on the right.'

'The one from which one can see the rear of Madame Birard's house?'

'Yes.'

'Your father was still at the village hall at that moment?'

'Yes.'

'Marcel said nothing?'

'No. He looked out of the window.'

'Do you know what he was looking at?'

'From my seat, I couldn't see.'

'Do you usually watch Marcel?'

'Yes,' he admitted, embarrassed.

This time, Maigret did not ask why. They were two good pupils and, because Jean-Paul was the teacher's son, the other one was top of the class. Marcel was an altar boy and wore a surplice on Sundays. Marcel had friends, had Joseph, the butcher's son, with whom he whispered during playtimes and at whose house he went to play after class.

'Did you see your father leave the village hall?'

'He walked towards our house and went inside to drink a cup of coffee.'

'Was the kitchen window open?'

'No. I know he had a cup of coffee. He always does.'

'Your mother was downstairs?'

'Upstairs, in my room. I could see her through the open window.'

'Your father, after that, did not go into the tool shed?'

'No. He crossed the courtyard to return to the classroom.'

'Marcel was still in front of the window, the one on the right?'

'Yes.'

'Why didn't you say so right away?'

'When?'

Maigret took the time to put his remembered evidence in order.

'Wait. Léonie Birard's body was discovered at the beginning of the afternoon. You children were not questioned right away?'

'We were not questioned that day. We didn't know exactly what was going on. We only saw people coming and going. Then we noticed the gendarmes.'

On Tuesday, in short, no one had openly accused the teacher. Marcel Sellier had not said anything, either to his parents or to anyone else. So Jean-Paul had no reason or chance to contradict him.

'Were you there, the next day, when they questioned Marcel?'

'No. They had us come to the office one by one.'

'And when he returned on Thursday morning? When did you learn that he claimed to have seen your father?'

'I don't remember any more.'

'On Tuesday evening did your parents talk about Léonie Birard?'

'Only after I was in bed. I heard part of what they were saying. My mother claimed that it was her fault. My father was saying that, no, it was only rumours, that they would understand that he'd had nothing to do with it.'

'Why, when you learned that Marcel was accusing him, did you not protest?'

'They wouldn't have believed me.'

Once again, Maigret thought he detected a nuance, a hint, something too subtle to be expressed. The youngster had not been glad to see his father accused. He had probably felt a certain shame at knowing he was in prison. But hadn't there been, on his part, a kind of cowardice? Hadn't he wanted, however slightly, without admitting it to himself, to distance himself from his parents?

He resented them for not being like other parents. Well, now they were more different from them than ever, and the village, instead of keeping them at a distance, was turning against them.

Jean-Paul envied Marcel.

Was he going to accuse him in turn?

In the end, he had not given in to a bad impulse. It was not cowardice, or in any case, not simply cowardice.

Couldn't one say that on the contrary, it was a form of loyalty towards the others?

He had the opportunity to contradict Marcel, to call him a liar. It was easy. Perhaps it seemed to him too easy, a cheap victory?

Besides, the fact remained that no one would believe him. Who would have, in the village, if he had shown up to say:

'Sellier lied. My father did not come out of the tool shed. I saw him go into the house, leave it and cross the courtyard. And at that moment, Marcel was in front of the opposite window, from which he couldn't see him.'

'You didn't say anything to your mother?'

'No.'

'Is she crying a lot?'

'She doesn't cry.'

That was worse. Maigret imagined the atmosphere in the house over the last few days.

'Why did you come out this morning?'

'To see.'

'To see Marcel?'

'Maybe.'

And perhaps, without realizing it, because of a need to participate, even from afar, in the life of the village? Wasn't he suffocating, in the little house at the end of the court-yard, where they no longer dared open the windows?

'Are you going to tell the lieutenant?'

'First I have to see Marcel.'

'Will you be telling him I was the one who said something?'

'Would you rather he didn't know that?'

'Yes.'

At heart, he had not completely given up on being admitted one day to the select group of Marcel, Joseph and the others.

'I believe he will tell me the truth without my needing to bring you into it. Other classmates must have seen which window he was standing at.'

'They were fooling around.'

'All of them?'

'Except for one of the girls, Louise Boncœur.'

'How old is she?'

'Fifteen.'

'She doesn't join in with the others?'

'No.'

'Do you think she was looking at Marcel?'

For the first time, his face flushed, especially the ears.

'She's always looking at him,' he stammered.

Was it because she was in love with the tinsmith's son that she had not contradicted him or, more simply, because she hadn't distinguished between one window and another? Marcel had affirmed that he had been standing near the window. His classmates had probably not thought about which window he meant.

'We should be getting back to the village,' observed the inspector.

'I would rather not go back there with you.'

'Do you want to leave first?'

'Yes. Are you sure you won't say anything to Marcel?'

Maigret nodded. The boy hesitated, touched his cap politely, began walking towards the meadows and soon broke into a run.

At the seashore at last, the inspector forgot to look at it and watched the figure moving away on the road.

He set out in turn, stopped to fill his pipe, blew his nose, grumbled unintelligibly, and anyone seeing him walk slowly on his way would doubtless have wondered why he was shaking his head every now and then.

By the time he passed the cemetery, the grave-diggers had finished covering Léonie Birard's coffin with yellowish earth, and thanks to the fresh bouquets and floral wreaths, her plot could be seen from a long way off.

7. The Doctor's Forbearance

The women had gone home and, save for a few who lived at distant farms, they had probably already changed out of their black dresses and good shoes. As for the men, they remained, as on a country-fair day, spilling out of Louis' inn on to the pavement and into the courtyard, where they could be seen setting their bottles on a window ledge or an old iron table that had spent the winter there.

From the pitch of the voices, the laughter, the slow clumsiness of the gestures, it was clear that they had had a lot to drink, and someone, whose face Maigret could not see, was relieving himself behind the hedge.

Thérèse, bustling about, had found a moment to hand him a glass and a carafe. Only a few steps inside, he was now surrounded by conversations and caught sight of the doctor in the kitchen, but there were too many people in the way for the inspector to get to him just then.

'I'd never have thought we'd be planting her in the ground,' an old man was saying, nodding his head.

There were three of them, of about the same age. All three were certainly over seventy-five and in their corner they were standing in front of the sign on the white wall posting the laws regarding public drunkenness and the sale of alcoholic beverages. Dressed in starched shirts and their black Sunday suits, they had to stand more stiffly than usual, which gave them a certain solemnity.

It was strange to discover, in their wrinkled and deeply creased faces, that when they looked at one another, their eyes took on a naive, childish expression. Each one was holding a glass. The tallest of the three, with magnificent white hair and a silky moustache, was swaying slightly and whenever he wanted to say something would place a finger on the shoulder of one of his companions.

Why did Maigret imagine them suddenly in the courtyard of the school? In their laughter and the glances they exchanged, they were still schoolboys. They had gone to classes together. Later, they had taken the same girls into the fields and attended one another's weddings, the funerals of their parents, the weddings of their children and the baptisms of their grandchildren.

'She might almost have been my sister, because my father always told me that he'd tumbled her mother in the haystack time and again. She was a hell of a female, it seems, and her husband was a cuckold his whole life.'

Didn't that just sum up the village? Behind Maigret, in another group, someone was holding forth.

'When he sold me that there cow, I told him: "Listen, Victor. I know you're a thief. But don't forget that we did our military service together in Montpellier, and that one evening . . ."'

Louis, who hadn't had time to change, had simply taken off his jacket. Maigret made his way along slowly, remembering that the doctor had invited him to lunch at home that day. Had Bresselles forgotten?

The doctor was holding a glass, like everyone else, but was keeping his head and trying to reason with the butcher, Marcellin, who was the drunkest man of all and apparently quite agitated. It was difficult, at that distance, to work out exactly what was happening. From what Maigret heard, Marcellin seemed to be railing against somebody, trying to push away the little doctor and get into the front room.

'I'm telling you I'm going to tell him!'

'Calm down, Marcellin. You're drunk.'

'I've got no right to be drunk, is it?'

'What did I tell you the last time you came for a check-up?'

'I don't give a damn!'

'If you keep this up, the next funeral will be yours.'

'I won't be spied on. I'm a free man.'

The wine was not doing him any favours. His face was white, with an unhealthy pink at the cheeks and eyelids. He could no longer control his movements. His voice was thickening.

'You hear me, sawbones? I can't stand spies. Well, what's he doing here, if not . . .'

It was Maigret he was looking at, back there, and towards whom he was attempting to rush to tell him exactly what he thought. Two or three other men were watching him and laughing.

Someone held out a glass, which the doctor seized first and poured out on the floor.

'Don't you see he's had enough, Firmin?'

Until then, there had been no arguments, no altercations.

Basically, they all knew one another too well to fight, and each man knew exactly who was the strongest. Maigret avoided getting any closer, pretending not to notice what was going on so as not to aggravate the butcher. He kept an eye on the group, however, and witnessed a scene he found not a little surprising.

The deputy mayor, Théo, tall and flabby, with his perpetually mocking eyes, now joined the others, brandishing a glass of not wine but a Pernod so dark it must have had quite a kick.

He spoke briefly and quietly to the doctor, then handed the glass to the butcher while placing a hand on his shoulder. He talked to him, too, and Marcellin at first appeared to struggle and be about to shove him away.

Finally, he grabbed the glass, which he drained in one go, and almost immediately his gaze grew muddled, dull. He tried again to point a threatening finger at the inspector, but his arm had grown too heavy. Then, as if he had just knocked him out, Théo pushed him towards the stairs, where, after a few steps up, he had to heave him on to his shoulder.

'You haven't forgotten my invitation, have you?'

The doctor, who had joined Maigret, was sighing with relief and said almost the same thing as the old man in the corner.

'*They've planted her in the ground!* Are you coming?'

They both made their way out to the pavement and walked a few paces along.

'Within three months, it will be Marcellin's turn. I keep telling him: "Marcellin, if you don't stop drinking, you'll croak!"

'He's reached the point where he's stopped eating.'

'He's ill?'

'They're all ill in his family. He's a sad case.'

'Did Théo go up to put him to bed?'

'We had to get rid of him somehow.'

He opened his door. The house smelled of good cooking.

'You'll have an aperitif?'

'I'd rather not.'

The smell of wine had been so strong in Louis' inn that simply breathing the air could have made a man drunk.

'Did you attend the funeral?'

'At a distance.'

'I looked for you coming out of the cemetery, but didn't see you. Is lunch ready, Armande?'

'In five minutes.'

Only two places were set. Just like a priest's servant, the doctor's sister preferred not to sit at the table. She must have eaten standing in her kitchen, between two courses.

'Sit down. What do you think of it?'

'Of what?'

'Nothing. Everything. She had a first-rate funeral!'

'The teacher is still in prison,' grumbled Maigret.

'They had to put someone there.'

'I'd like to ask you a question, doctor. Among all those people at the funeral, do you think there were many who believe that Gastin killed Léonie Birard?'

'A few of them, surely. There are people who'll believe anything.'

'And the rest?'

The doctor did not immediately grasp Maigret's point.

'Let's say that a tenth of the population is convinced that the teacher fired the gun,' began the inspector.

'That's about right.'

'The other nine-tenths have their own ideas.'

'No doubt about that.'

'Whom do they suspect?'

'It depends. In my opinion, each of them suspects more or less sincerely the person they'd most like to be guilty.'

'And no one is talking about it?'

'They must be, among themselves.'

'Have you heard of any suspicions along those lines?'

The ironic look the doctor gave him might almost have come from Théo.

'They don't tell me that sort of thing.'

'Yet knowing or believing that the teacher is not guilty, it doesn't bother them that he's in prison.'

'Certainly not. Gastin is not from the village. They feel that if the lieutenant and the examining magistrate have judged it wise to arrest him, that's their business. That's what they're both paid to do.'

'They'd let him be convicted?'

'Without batting an eye. If it were one of theirs, then that would be a different story. Are you beginning to understand? Once a guilty culprit is required, it might as well be a stranger.'

'Do they think the Sellier boy is sincere?'

'Marcel is a good boy.'

'He lied.'

'It's possible.'

'I wonder why.'

'Perhaps because he thought they were going to accuse his father. Don't forget, his mother is the old Birard woman's niece, and she'll be the heir.'

'I thought the postmistress had always claimed that her niece would not get a thing.'

The doctor looked a touch uneasy. His sister brought in the appetizers.

'Were you at the funeral?' Maigret asked her.

'Armande never goes to funerals.'

They began to eat in silence. It was Maigret who first spoke again, as if talking to himself.

'It was not Tuesday, but Monday, that Marcel Sellier saw the teacher leave the tool shed.'

'He has admitted it?'

'I haven't asked him yet, but I'm almost certain of it. On Monday, before school, Gastin worked in his garden. When he crossed the courtyard sometime that morning, he noticed a hoe lying around and went to put it away. On Tuesday evening, after the discovery of the body, Marcel said nothing and was not yet thinking of accusing his teacher.

'Later, he had an idea, or overheard something in conversation that made up his mind to it.

'He did not lie completely. Women and children specialize in these half-lies. He did not make anything up, simply moved a real event one day later.'

'That's rather funny!'

'I would bet he's trying to persuade himself that it really was Tuesday when he saw the teacher come out of the shed. He can't manage it, obviously, so he must have gone to confession.'

'Why don't you ask the priest?'

'Because if he were to answer me, it would indirectly betray the secrets of the confessional. The priest won't do that. I was thinking of asking the neighbours, the people in the cooperative, among others, if they had seen Marcel enter the church at a time when there was no service, but now I know that he goes there through the courtyard.'

The leg of lamb was perfection, and the beans meltingly tender. The doctor had brought out a vintage bottle. Outside, they could hear a muffled noise, the sound of conversation on the square and in the courtyard of the inn.

Did the doctor realize that Maigret was only talking to try out his ideas on an audience? He was circling around the same subject, lazily, without ever getting to the essential point.

'In the end, I don't think Marcel lied to deflect any suspicion from his father.'

The inspector had the feeling, at that moment, that Bresselles knew more than he wanted to say.

'Really?'

'I'm trying, you see, to put myself in the place of the children. Since the beginning, I've had the impression that it's all about the children, and the grown-ups have become involved in it only by accident.'

Looking the doctor full in the face, he added calmly, pointedly:

'And I believe more and more that others know this as well.'

'Perhaps, in that case, you will succeed in making them talk?'

'Perhaps. It's difficult, isn't it?'

'Very.'

Bresselles was making fun of him, still in the same way as the deputy mayor did.

'I had, this morning, a long conversation with the Gastin boy.'

'Did you go to their house?'

'No. I spotted him watching the funeral over the cemetery wall and followed him all the way to the sea.'

'Why was he going there?'

'He was running away from me. At the same time, he was hoping I would catch him.'

'What did he tell you?'

'That Marcel Sellier was standing not at the left-hand window, but at the one on the right. At most, Marcel could have seen Léonie Birard fall at the moment the bullet entered her eye, but he could not possibly have seen the teacher coming out of the shed.'

'What do you conclude?'

'That it was to shield someone that the Sellier boy decided to lie. Not right away. He took his time. The idea probably did not occur to him immediately.'

'Why did he pick the teacher?'

'First, because he was the most likely person. And also, as it happened, because he had seen him the day before, almost at the same time, coming out of the shed. Finally, perhaps because of Jean-Paul.'

'Do you think he hates him?'

'Mind you, doctor, I'm not affirming anything. I'm feeling my way. I've questioned the two children. This morning I watched some old men who were once children as well, in this very place. If the inhabitants of the village are so easily hostile to strangers, isn't it because, without their knowing it, they envy them? They spend their entire existence in Saint-André, with the occasional trip to La Rochelle or the distraction of a wedding or a funeral.'

'I see what you're driving at.'

'The teacher comes from Paris. In their eyes, he's a learned man, who busies himself with their personal doings and intrudes on them with his advice. For a child, the teacher's son has a little of the same prestige.'

'Marcel lied because he hates Jean-Paul?'

'Partly because he envies him. The strangest thing is that, for his part, Jean-Paul envies Marcel and his friends. He feels alone, different from the others, kept at a distance by them.'

'Nevertheless, someone shot at the old Birard woman, and it couldn't have been either of those two boys.'

'That's right.'

A home-made apple tart arrived, and the smell of coffee wafted in from the kitchen.

'I'm beginning to feel that Théo knows the truth.'

'Because he was in his garden?'

'For that and other reasons. Yesterday evening, doctor, you told me gaily that they're all a bunch of crooks.'

'I was joking.'

'Half-joking, isn't that so? They all cheat, more or less,

committing what you would call nasty little tricks. You have your blunt manner. You scold them on occasion. But in reality, you would not betray them. Am I right?'

'The priest, according to you, would refuse to answer you if you were to question him about Marcel, and I think you're right. Me, I'm their doctor. It's somewhat the same thing. Do you know, inspector, that our lunch is beginning to resemble an interrogation? What do you prefer with your coffee? Brandy or calvados?'

'Calvados.'

Bresselles went to fetch the bottle from an antique cabinet and filled the glasses, still pleasant and cheerful, but with a slightly more serious look in his eyes.

'Your health.'

'I would like to talk to you about the accident,' began Maigret, almost timidly.

'What accident?'

The doctor's question was simply to give himself time to think, for accidents were not that frequent in the village.

'The motorbike accident.'

'Has someone told you about it?'

'I know only that Marcellin's son was knocked down by a motorbike. When did it happen?'

'A little more than a month ago, on a Saturday.'

'Near Léonie Birard's house?'

'Not far from it. Maybe a hundred metres away.'

'During the evening?'

'A bit before dinner. It was dark. The two boys . . .'

'Which boys?'

'Marcel and Joseph, Marcellin's son.'

'Just the two of them?'

'Yes. They were going home. A motorbike was coming from the seashore. No one knows exactly how it happened.'

'Who was the motorcyclist?'

'Hervé Jusseau, a mussel-farmer of about thirty who got married last year.'

'He'd been drinking?'

'He doesn't drink. He was raised by his aunts, who are quite strict and who still live with the family.'

'Was his headlamp on?'

'The investigation showed that it was. The children must have been playing. Joseph tried to cross the road and was knocked down.'

'Was his leg broken?'

'In two places.'

'Will he limp?'

'No. In a week or two, it'll be like new.'

'He still can't walk yet?'

'No.'

'Does the accident bring in something for Marcellin?'

'The insurance will pay a certain sum, because Jusseau admitted that he was probably at fault.'

'Do you think that he was?'

Visibly uncomfortable, the doctor decided to burst out laughing.

'I'm beginning to understand what you call, at Quai des Orfèvres, sweating a witness. I would rather 'fess up. Isn't that how you put it?'

He refilled the glasses.

'Marcellin is a poor wretch. Everyone knows he's not going to last much longer. We can't hold it against him that he drinks, because he has never had any luck. Not only has there always been illness in his house, but everything he tries goes wrong. Three years ago he rented some meadows to fatten bullocks, and a drought took everything. He's always hard up. His van spends more time broken down by the roadside than it does delivering meat.'

'So Jusseau, who has nothing to lose, since the insurance is paying, said he was at fault?'

'That's about it.'

'Does everyone know this?'

'More or less. An insurance company is a vague and distant entity, like the government, and it always seems only right to take money from it.'

'Did you draw up the medical certificates?'

'Of course.'

'Did you formulate them in such a way that Marcellin would receive as much as possible?'

'Let's say that I emphasized the complications that might arise.'

'There weren't any complications?'

'There could have been. When a cow dies of a sudden sickness, five times out of ten the veterinarian writes it up as an accident.'

It was Maigret's turn to smile.

'If I understand correctly, Marcellin's son could have been back on his feet a week or two ago.'

'One week.'

'By keeping him in a cast, you're allowing his father to claim a larger sum from the insurance company?'

'You see that even the doctor is obliged to be a bit crooked. If I'd refused, I would have been long gone from here. And the teacher is clearly in prison today because he refused to provide such certifications. If he'd been more flexible, if he hadn't fought a hundred times with Théo over his being too generous with government money, they might have adopted him in the end.'

'In spite of what happened to his wife?'

'They've all been cheated on too.'

'Was Marcel Sellier the only witness to the accident?'

'I told you, it was in the evening. There was no one else on the road.'

'Could someone have seen them from a window?'

'You're thinking of the old Birard woman?'

'I assume that she wasn't *always* in her kitchen and that she sometimes went into the front room.'

'She never came up in the investigation. She didn't say anything.'

The doctor scratched his head, completely serious, this time.

'I have the feeling you're closing in on where you're going. Mind you, I'm not following you yet.'

'You're sure of that?'

'Of what?'

'Why did Marcellin try to rush at me this morning?'

'He was drunk.'

'Why come after me, in particular?'

'You were the only stranger in the inn. When he's been drinking, he feels persecuted. From there to imagining that you're here only to spy on him . . .'

'You went to some trouble to calm him down.'

'You would have preferred a fight?'

'Théo knocked him out by making him drink a double or triple Pernod and carried him upstairs. That's the first time I've seen the deputy mayor ride to the rescue.'

'Marcellin is his cousin.'

'I'd rather he'd been allowed to tell me what he wanted to say.'

The others had clearly not wanted him to speak, had whisked him away, in effect, and now the butcher must have been sleeping it off in one of the upstairs bedrooms.

'I'm going to have to go to my surgery,' said Bresselles. 'I've probably got a good dozen people waiting for me.'

The two rooms of his office were in a low building, in the courtyard. Patients could be seen sitting there in a row against a wall, including a child with a bandaged head and an old man with crutches.

'I think you'll get somewhere!' said the little doctor with a sigh, alluding to Maigret's investigation, of course, not his career.

He considered the inspector now with a certain respect, but also with a hint of irritation.

'You would have preferred that I find nothing?'

'I wonder. It might have been better if you'd never come.'

'That depends on what there is at the end. You haven't the slightest idea about that?'

'I know about as much as you do.'

'And you would have left Gastin in prison?'

'In any case, they can't keep him very long.'

Bresselles was not a local man. He had been born in a city, like the teacher. But for more than twenty years he had been living with the village and, in spite of himself, he felt a part of it.

'Come see me when you feel like it. Believe me, I do what I can. It simply happens that I would rather live here and spend most of my days on the local roads than shut myself up in a consulting room in a city or some suburb.'

'Thank you for the lunch.'

'Will you question young Marcel again?'

'I don't know yet.'

'If you want him to talk, it would be better if you saw him without his father present.'

'Is he afraid of his father?'

'I don't think that it's fear. Admiration, rather. If he lied, he must be living in terror.'

Back outside, Maigret found only a few groups left in the square and at the Bon Coin. Théo was playing cards in a corner, as on other days, with the postman, the blacksmith and a farmer. His eyes met Maigret's and, although as mocking as before, they were beginning to reflect a certain respect.

'Is Marcellin still upstairs?' the inspector asked Thérèse.

'He's snoring! He's soiled the entire room. He can't hold his drink any more. It's the same thing every time.'

'Has anyone asked for me?'

'The lieutenant came by a little while ago. He didn't come in, only glanced inside as if looking for someone, maybe you. Are you having anything?'

'No, thanks.'

Even the smell of wine was nauseating. He headed slowly for the village hall. One of the sergeants was talking with Lieutenant Daniélou.

'Did you try to see me?'

'Not particularly. I went through the square a while ago and looked to see if you were at the inn.'

'Anything new?'

'It might not be important. Sergeant Nouli has found another rifle.'

'A .22 calibre?'

'Yes. Here it is. It's the same type as the others.'

'Where was it?'

'In the shed behind the butcher's house.'

'Hidden?'

The sergeant replied himself.

'I was still busy looking for the spent cartridge with my colleague. We were going from one garden to the next. I saw the door of a shed open, with bloodstains everywhere. In a corner, I spotted the rifle.'

'Did you question the butcher's wife?'

'Yes. She told me that, when Sellier beat the town drum to ask that all rifles be brought to the village hall, she hadn't thought of her son's rifle, given that he was laid up in bed. He had an accident a month ago and . . .'

'I know.'

Maigret, holding the weapon, was taking little puffs on his pipe. He finally placed the rifle in a separate corner from the others.

'Would you come with me for a moment, lieutenant?'

They crossed the courtyard, pushed open the door of the classroom, which smelled of chalk and ink.

'Keep in mind that I don't know yet where this will take us. On Tuesday morning, when the teacher left here with the farmer Piedbœuf, Marcel Sellier went to this window.'

'That is what he told us.'

'We can see, to the right of the linden, the tool shed. We can also see some windows, including those on the first floor of the butcher's house.'

Frowning slightly, the lieutenant listened.

'The boy did not stay here. Before the teacher left the village hall office, the boy crossed the classroom.'

Maigret did so as well, passing in front of the blackboard, the teacher's desk, heading for the window directly opposite the first one.

'From here, as you can confirm, we see Léonie Birard's house. If she was standing at her window when she was hit, as the inquiry seems to indicate, it is possible that Marcel saw her fall.'

'Do you suppose he had a reason for going from one window to the other? He might have seen something and . . .'

'Not necessarily.'

'Why did he lie?'

Maigret preferred not to answer.

'You have your suspicions?'

'I think so.'

'What are you going to do?'

'What there is to do,' replied Maigret flatly.

He sighed, emptied his pipe on the greyish floor, looked at the ashes there with an air of reluctance and added, as if with regret:

'It's not going to be pleasant.'

Directly across the courtyard, from a window on the first floor, Jean-Paul was watching them.

8. Léonie's Horseshoe

Before leaving the classroom, Maigret saw another form at a window, an open one this time, further away, beyond the gardens. The person sitting on the window-sill had his back turned, but from the shape of his head and his sturdy build Maigret recognized Marcel Sellier.

'I suppose that's the butcher's house?'

'Yes . . . Joseph, the son, and Marcel are great friends.'

Across the way, the boy twisted around on the sill, then looked down to watch a woman hanging laundry out to dry in a garden. He glanced automatically about the yard just at the moment when Maigret and the lieutenant were leaving the classroom and facing his way.

In spite of the distance, one could tell from his movements that he was talking to someone in the room. He then got down off the window-sill and disappeared.

Turning towards the inspector, Daniélou murmured pensively:

'Good luck.'

'Are you returning to La Rochelle?'

'Would you prefer that I wait for you?'

'That might allow me to take the evening train.'

He had no more than 150 metres to cross. He did so in long, even strides. The butcher's shop was a low, huddled house. There was no real shop; it was the left-hand room on the ground floor, which had been adapted by adding a strange sort of counter with a scale, an old-model ice box and a table for cutting meat.

The front door opened to a hallway, the end of which, to the left of the staircase, opened on to the courtyard.

Before knocking, Maigret had passed the right-hand window, the one in the kitchen; it was open, showing three women, including an elderly lady in a white bonnet, sitting at a round table eating some pie. One of them must have been Marcellin's wife, the two others her mother and sister, who lived in the neighbouring village and had come for the funeral.

They had seen him pass by. The windows were so small that he had blocked theirs for a moment with his burly torso. They heard him hesitating at the open door, looking for a bell, not finding one and taking two steps inside, making noise on purpose.

The butcher's wife rose, half-opened the kitchen door and asked:

'What is it?'

Then, probably recognizing him from seeing him around the village:

'You're the policeman from Paris, aren't you?'

If she had gone to the funeral, she had already changed her clothes. She couldn't have been very old, yet her shoulders were bowed, her cheeks hollow and her eyes feverish.

'My husband isn't here,' she added, without looking him in the face. 'I don't know when he'll be back. Were you wanting to see him?'

She did not invite him in to the kitchen, where the other two women sat in silence.

'I would like a word with your son.'

She was afraid, but that meant nothing, for she was a woman who must always have been afraid, who lived in the expectation of catastrophe.

'He's in bed.'

'I know.'

'He's been upstairs for more than a month.'

'May I go up?'

What could she do? She let him pass without daring to protest, clutching a corner of her apron. He had climbed only four or five steps when he saw Marcel coming down the same stairs, and it was Maigret who now pressed back against the wall.

'Excuse me . . .' stammered the boy, who also avoided looking straight at him.

He was hurrying to get outside, must have expected Maigret to stop him on his way or call him back, but the inspector did not and went on upstairs.

'The door to the right,' the mother told him when he reached the landing.

He knocked.

'Come in,' said a child's voice.

The mother stayed there, motionless, her face lifted towards him as he pushed open the door and closed it behind him.

'Don't bother.'

Sitting on his bed, propped up by several pillows, one leg in plaster up to mid-thigh, Joseph had moved as if to get up.

'I passed your friend on the stairs.'

'I know.'

'Why didn't he wait for me?'

The ceiling was low, and Maigret almost touched the main beam with his head. The room was not large. The bed took up most of it. The place was untidy, littered with illustrated magazines and bits of wood carved with a pocketknife.

'Bored, are you?'

There was a chair, but it was heaped with various things: a jacket, a slingshot, two or three books and more pieces of wood.

'You can take everything off it,' said the boy.

Jean-Paul Gastin resembled his father and mother. Marcel resembled the tinsmith.

Joseph, though, looked neither like the butcher nor his wife. Of the three children, he was without question the handsomest, the one who seemed most like a healthy, well-adjusted child.

Maigret had gone to sit on the window-sill, his back to the landscape of courtyards and gardens, in the place where Marcel had recently been sitting, and he was in no hurry to talk. This was not, as so often happened with him at Quai des Orfèvres, intended to unnerve another person, but because he had no idea where to begin.

Joseph spoke first.

'Where is my father?'

'At Louis' place.'

The child hesitated before his next question.

'How is he?'

What point was there in hiding what he must certainly have known?

'Théo put him to bed.'

Instead of worried, he seemed comforted by the news.

'Is my mother downstairs with my grandmother?'

'Yes.'

The sun, setting in a still-clear sky, gently warmed the inspector's back, and birdsong rose from the gardens. Somewhere, a child was playing a tin trumpet.

'Don't you want me to take off your plaster cast?'

It was as if Joseph expected that, understanding the implication. He was not worried, like his mother. He did not seem afraid. Studying the bulky form of his visitor and his seemingly impassive face, he thought about what tack to take.

'You know about that?'

'Yes.'

'The doctor told you?'

'I'd guessed earlier. What were you doing, you and Marcel, when the motorbike hit you?'

Joseph was truly relieved.

'Didn't you find the horseshoe?' he asked.

And those words brought an image to Maigret's mind. He had seen a horseshoe somewhere. It was when he had visited Léonie Birard's house. The rusty horseshoe had been lying on the floor, in the corner to the right of the window, not far from the chalk lines marking the position of the body.

It hadn't escaped him. He had even almost asked a question. Then, straightening up, he had noticed a nail, had told himself that the shoe had probably been hanging up on this nail. Lots of people out in the country keep a horseshoe they've found on the road as a good-luck charm.

Daniélou and the gendarmes who had already examined the premises must have thought the same thing.

'There is indeed a horseshoe in Léonie Birard's place,' he replied.

'I'm the one who found it,' said the boy, 'the night of the accident. I was on the sea road with Marcel when I tripped over it. It was dark. I took the horseshoe with me. We were passing the old lady's house, and I had it in my hand. The window on the street side was open. We went over, without making any noise.'

'Was the postmistress in the front room?'

'In the kitchen. The door was ajar.'

He could not keep from smiling.

'First I had the idea of throwing the horseshoe into the house to scare her.'

'The way you used to throw in dead cats and other filth?'

'I'm not the only one who did that.'

'You changed your mind?'

'Yes. I thought it would be funnier to sneak the horseshoe into her bed. I climbed quietly through the window, took a few steps; unfortunately, I bumped into something, I don't know what. She heard. I dropped the horseshoe and jumped out of the window.'

'Where was Marcel?'

'He was waiting a little further along. I started to run.

I heard the old woman shouting threats from her window, and that's when the motorbike hit me.'

'Why didn't you say so?'

'First off, they took me to the doctor, and it hurt a lot. They gave me some medicine that put me to sleep. When I woke up, my father was there and the first thing they talked about was the insurance. I understood that if I told the truth, people would say it was my fault, and the insurance wouldn't pay. My father needs money.'

'Marcel came to see you?'

'Yes. I made him promise not to say anything, either.'

'Since then, he's been by to see you every day?'

'Almost every day. He's my friend.'

'Jean-Paul isn't your friend?'

'He isn't anyone's friend.'

'Why?'

'I don't know. He probably doesn't want it. He's like his mother. His mother never speaks to the women in the village.'

'Aren't you bored, alone in this bedroom for a month?'

'Yes.'

'What do you do all day?'

'Nothing. I read. I whittle pieces of wood and make little boats and people out of them.'

There were dozens of them around him, some rather carefully done.

'Do you ever go over to the window?'

'I'm not supposed to.'

'For fear people would find out you can walk?'

'Yes,' he replied frankly. Then he asked, 'Are you going to tell the insurance company?'

'That's none of my business.'

There was a silence, during which Maigret turned around to look at the schoolyard and the backs of the houses.

'I suppose that it's especially during playtime that you look out of the window?'

'Often.'

Exactly opposite, beyond the little gardens, he could see the windows of Léonie Birard.

'Did the postmistress happen to see you?'

'Yes.'

The child became more subdued, now, still hesitating a bit, but knew already that he would have to talk.

'Already, before, when she saw me she would make faces at me.'

'Did she stick out her tongue at you?'

'Yes. After the accident, she began taunting me, showing me the horseshoe.'

'Why?'

'Probably to make me understand that she could go and tell everything.'

'Yet she did not do that.'

'No.'

It was a little as if the former postmistress had been the same age as the youngsters with whom she used to squabble and who had targeted her for their teasing. She would shout, threaten, stick out her tongue at them. At a distance, she was reminding Joseph that she could cause trouble for him.

'Did that scare you?'

'Yes. My parents need money.'

'Do they know about the business with the horseshoe?'

'My father does.'

'You told him about it?'

'He guessed that I had done something that I wasn't telling him and made me admit the truth.'

'Did he scold you?'

'He advised me to keep quiet.'

'How many times did Léonie Birard show you the horseshoe in the window?'

'Maybe twenty times. She did it whenever she saw me.'

As he had done on the morning with Jean-Paul, Maigret slowly lit his pipe, so as to appear as unthreatening as possible. He seemed to be listening distractedly to some story or other, and, seeing him relaxing, with an almost naive expression, the boy might have imagined that he was chatting with one of his classmates.

'What did Marcel come to tell you a little while ago?'

'That if he were questioned again, he'd have to own up.'

'Why? Is he frightened?'

'He went to confession. I also think the funeral scared him.'

'He'll say he saw you at this window before going over to the one on the other side?'

'How did you know? You see! In this house, everything goes wrong. Other people do worse things, and nothing happens to them. In our house, it's the exact opposite.'

'What were you doing at the window?'

'I was looking.'

'Was the old lady showing you the horseshoe?'

'Yes.'

'Tell me exactly what happened.'

'There's nothing else I can do, right?'

'Not at this point.'

'I took my rifle.'

'Where was your rifle?'

'In that corner there, near the wardrobe.'

'Was it loaded?'

There was the slightest hesitation.

'Yes.'

'Were the cartridges .22 longs or shorts?'

'Longs.'

'Do you usually keep the rifle in your bedroom?'

'Often.'

'Have you happened to shoot at sparrows from the window lately?'

The boy paused again, thinking as fast as he could, like someone who cannot allow himself the tiniest mistake.

'No. I don't think so.'

'Did you want to frighten the old woman?'

'Probably. I don't know exactly what I wanted. She was making fun of me. I thought in the end she'd tell the insurance company and that my father wouldn't be able to buy himself a new van.'

'That's what he decided to do with the money?'

'Yes. He's sure that if he had a good van and could extend his route, he would earn some money.'

'He isn't earning any at the moment?'

'He's been losing money for months, and it's my grand-mother who . . .'

'She's helping you?'

'When it's absolutely necessary. She makes a scene every time.'

'You fired the rifle?'

He nodded, with a vague, apologetic smile.

'Aiming at anything?'

'I was aiming at the window.'

'In short, you wanted to break a pane of glass?'

He nodded again, and asked hurriedly:

'Will they put me in prison?'

'They don't put boys your age in prison.'

He seemed disappointed.

'Then what will they do?'

'The judge will lecture you.'

'And after that?'

'He'll speak sternly to your father. He's the one, in the end, who is responsible.'

'Why, since he didn't do anything?'

'Where was he, when you fired?'

'I don't know.'

'Was he off on his rounds?'

'Probably not. He never leaves that early.'

'Was he in the butcher shop?'

'Maybe.'

'He didn't hear anything? Your mother didn't, either?'

'No. They didn't say anything to me.'

'They don't know that you're the one who fired the shot?'

'I didn't tell them about it.'

'Who took the rifle to the shed?'

This time he blushed, glanced around uneasily and would not look Maigret in the eyes.

'I assume,' insisted the inspector, 'that you could not go downstairs and cross the courtyard in your cast. So?'

'I asked Marcel . . .'

He stopped short.

'No. That's not true,' he admitted. 'It was my father. You'd find it out in the end, anyway.'

'Did you ask him to take down the rifle?'

'Yes. I didn't explain why to him.'

'When?'

'Wednesday morning.'

'Didn't he ask you any questions?'

'He just looked at me with annoyance.'

'He didn't mention it to your mother?'

'If he had, she would have come immediately to worm things out of me.'

'She has the habit of doing that?'

'She always guesses when I try to lie.'

'Are you the one who asked Marcel to claim that he'd seen the teacher come out of the tool shed?'

'No. I didn't even know he would be questioned.'

'Why did he do it?'

'Probably because he saw me at the window.'

'With the rifle. Were you holding the rifle?'

Joseph was flushed; he was making valiant efforts, trying his best not to contradict himself or appear to be hesitating.

Although Maigret was speaking to him in a neutral voice, without pressing him, as if he were saying nothing important, the boy was intelligent enough to realize that he was moving ever closer towards the truth.

'I don't remember exactly. Maybe I hadn't already picked it up.'

'But when Marcel was at the other window and saw the postmistress falling, did he suspect that you had fired the shot?'

'He didn't tell me that.'

'The two of you didn't talk about it?'

'Not until today.'

'And he simply announced that, if he were questioned, he'd be obliged to admit the truth?'

'Yes.'

'Was he sad?'

'Yes.'

'And you?'

'I'd rather get it over with.'

'But would you rather go to prison?'

'Maybe.'

'Why?'

'No reason. To see.'

He did not add that prison was doubtless more fun than his parents' house.

Maigret rose with a sigh.

'You would have let the teacher be convicted?'

'I don't think so.'

'Are you sure about that?'

No. Joseph was not sure about that. That he had wronged Gastin seemed not to have occurred to him. Had it occurred to the other villagers?

'Are you leaving?' asked the boy in astonishment, seeing the inspector walk towards the door. Maigret stopped at the threshold.

'What else would I do?'

'Are you going to tell the lieutenant everything?'

'Except, perhaps, the business about your accident.'

'Thank you.'

He wasn't that happy about being left alone.

'I suppose you have nothing to add?'

He shook his head.

'You're sure that you've told me the truth?'

He nodded again and then, instead of opening the door, Maigret sat down on the edge of the bed.

'Now, tell me *exactly* what you saw in the courtyard.'

'Which courtyard?'

The blood had rushed to the child's face, and his ears were crimson.

Before replying, Maigret opened the door a little, without having to get up, and told Marcellin's wife, standing out on the landing:

'Please be kind enough to go downstairs.'

After she had done so, he closed the door.

'In this courtyard.'

'Our courtyard?'

'Yes.'

'What would I have seen?'

'I'm not the one who knows. You are.'

The child, in his bed, had drawn back to the wall and was staring wild-eyed at Maigret.

'What do you mean?'

'You were at the window and the old lady was showing you the horseshoe.'

'I already told you.'

'Except that the rifle was not in your room.'

'How do you know?'

'Your father was downstairs, in the yard, with the door to the shed open. What was he doing?'

'Cutting up a lamb.'

'From his position, he could see you at your window, the way he could see Léonie Birard.'

'No one could have told you all that,' murmured the youngster, more dazzled than stunned. 'Did you simply guess?'

'He was on no better terms than you were with the old woman. She insulted him every time he went by on the road.'

'She called him a good-for-nothing and a beggar.'

'Did she stick her tongue out at him?'

'That was her favourite thing.'

'Did your father go into the shed?'

'Yes.'

'When he came back out, was he holding your rifle?'

'What will they do to him?'

'It depends. Have you made up your mind not to lie to me any more?'

'I'll tell you the truth.'

'Could your father still see you in the window at that moment?'

'I don't think so. I'd stepped back.'

'So that he wouldn't know you were watching?'

'Maybe. I don't remember. It happened very fast.'

'What happened very fast?'

'He took a quick look around and fired. I heard him mutter, "Take this, you old louse!"'

'Did he aim carefully?'

'No. He put the gun to his shoulder and fired.'

'Is he a good shot?'

'He couldn't hit a sparrow at ten paces.'

'Did he see Léonie Birard fall?'

'Yes. He froze for a moment, maybe completely shocked. Then he dashed into the shed to put away the rifle.'

'And after that?'

'He looked at my window and went inside the house. Then I heard him going out.'

'To go where?'

'To have a drink at Louis' place.'

'How do you know?'

'Because when he came home, he was drunk.'

'Théo was in his garden?'

'He had just come out of his shed.'

'Did he see your father shoot?'

'He couldn't have, from where he was.'

'But he saw you at the window?'

'I think so.'

'Did he hear the shot?'

'He must have heard it.'

'Your father hasn't mentioned anything since?'

'No.'

'You haven't talked to him either?'

'I didn't dare.'

'Did Marcel think you were the one who fired?'

'Surely.'

'That's why he lied?'

'I'm his friend.'

Maigret patted him absently on the head.

'That's all, little fellow!' he said as he stood up.

He almost added: 'Some people learn about life sooner than others.'

Why bother? Joseph wasn't taking the whole thing too tragically. He was so used to little daily dramas that this one, in his eyes, was hardly more impressive than the rest.

'They're going to put him in prison?'

'Not for long. Unless they prove that he aimed at Léonie Birard and tried to hit her.'

'He just wanted to scare her.'

'I know. The whole village will testify in his favour.'

After thinking it over, the boy agreed.

'I think so, yes. They do like him, in spite of everything. It's not his fault.'

'What isn't his fault?'

'Everything.'

Maigret was halfway down the stairs when the child called down to him.

'Don't you want to take off my cast?'

'It would be better if I sent the doctor over to you.'

'Will you send him over right away?'

'If he's at home.'

'Don't forget.'

Finally, when Maigret reached the bottom of the stairs, he heard a murmured:

'Thank you.'

He did not stop at the kitchen. The sun was sinking behind the houses, and mist was rising from the ground. The three women were still there, motionless, and silently watched him go past the window.

The priest was talking with a middle-aged woman in front of the church, and the inspector thought he seemed tempted to cross the street and speak to him. He must know, too. He knew from Marcel's confession of his lie. But he was the only one without the right to say anything.

When Maigret nodded in greeting, the priest appeared a bit surprised. Then the inspector entered the village hall, where he found Daniélou waiting for him, smoking a cigar. He looked up expectantly.

'You can release the teacher,' said Maigret.

'It's Joseph?'

Maigret shook his head.

'Who?'

'His father, Marcellin.'

'I assume all that's left is for me to arrest him?'

'I'll have a word or two with him first.'

'He didn't confess?'

'He's not in any condition to confess anything whatsoever. If you would come with me . . .'

They both headed for the inn, but, just at the door, Maigret remembered a promise he had made and went to ring at Doctor Bresselles' house.

The sister opened the door.

'Is the doctor in?'

'He just left to deliver a baby.'

'When he returns, would you ask him to go and remove Joseph's cast?'

She, too, must have thought that Joseph was the culprit.

The lieutenant was waiting at Louis' door. There was no longer anyone outside. A dozen or so drinkers still lingered inside, one of them sleeping with his head on a table.

'Where did they put Marcellin?' Maigret asked Thérèse.

He had spoken loudly enough for Théo to hear. And it was the inspector's turn to consider the deputy mayor with an eye twinkling with mischief. Théo, moreover, was a good sport. Instead of scowling, he simply shrugged as if to say:

'Too bad! It's not my fault . . .'

'The room to the left of the stairs, Monsieur Maigret.'

He went up, alone, and opened the door; startled by the noise, the butcher sat up and looked at him with bulging eyes.

'What do you want, you?' he said thickly. 'What time is it?'

'Five o'clock.'

He put both feet on the floor, rubbed his eyes, his face, then looked around him for something to drink. His breath was so rank with alcohol that Maigret felt nauseated, and there were patches of vomit on the floor.

'The lieutenant is waiting for you downstairs, Marcellin.'

'Me? Why? What have I done?'

'He'll tell you himself.'

'You went to my house?'

Maigret did not reply.

'You hassled the boy?' the butcher went on in a dull voice.

'Get up, Marcellin.'

'If I feel like it.'

His hair was mussed; his eyes, fixed in a stare.

'Well, aren't you the clever one! You must be proud of yourself! Tormenting children! That's what you came here to do! . . . And that's the kind of work the government pays you for!'

'Downstairs.'

'Don't you dare touch me.'

On his feet, swaying, he was muttering.

'All this because that other fellow's a teacher, because he's an educated man who gets the taxpayers' money, too . . .'

To emphasize his disdain, he spat on the floor, then made for the door and almost fell down the stairs.

'A Pernod, Louis!' he ordered, clinging to the counter.

Needing to go out with a flourish, he gazed at those around him while attempting to sneer.

With a look, Louis asked Maigret whether to serve the drink, and the inspector shrugged with indifference.

Marcellin downed his Pernod in one gulp, wiped his lips, turned towards Théo and cried:

'Anyway, I got her, that lousy stinker!'

'Well, don't go around boasting about it,' murmured the deputy mayor, consulting the cards in his hand.

'What, you're saying I didn't get her?'

'You didn't do it on purpose. You couldn't hit an ox at thirty metres.'

'Did I get her, yes or no?'

'You got her, fine! Now, shut up.'

The lieutenant stepped in.

'I ask you to come quietly, so I won't need to use handcuffs.'

'And if I feel like being handcuffed?'

He was showing off to the end.

'As you please.'

The others saw them gleam, heard them snap closed around the butcher's wrists.

'You see that, all of you?'

He bumped into the door frame as he left, and a few moments later they heard a car door slam shut.

There was silence. The air was steeped in wine and liquor; thick smoke surrounded the lamp, which had just been lit despite the lingering daylight outside. In half an hour, it would be completely dark, and the village would have dwindled to a few bright spots, two or three dimly lit shop windows and the occasional shadow slipping past the houses.

'Draw up my bill,' said Maigret, the first to speak.

'You're leaving right away?'

'I'm taking the evening train.'

The others remained quiet, as if in suspense.

'How do I go about calling a taxi?'

'Simply ask Marchandeau. He'll take you in his van. He's always the one who drives people to the station.'

'Are we playing,' demanded Théo, 'or not? I said spades were trumps. And here's three in a row.'

'On what?'

'The queen.'

'Good.'

'I'm playing the jack.'

Maigret seemed a little sad, or tired, as he did almost every time he had finished an investigation. He had come there to eat oysters washed down with the local white wine.

'What may I offer you, inspector? My treat.'

He hesitated. The odour of cheap wine was sickening. Still, because he'd so looked forward to it in Paris, he went along.

'A carafe of white.'

The lights were on in the ironmonger's shop. At the back, hung with buckets and saucepans, Marcel Sellier could be glimpsed sitting before a book in the kitchen, his head in his hands.

'Cheers!'

'Cheers!'

'You must have a strange idea of this place, no?'

He made no reply, and shortly afterwards Thérèse brought down his suitcase, which she had packed for him.

'I hope your wife will find everything in order.'

And in fact it was good, all of a sudden, to think of Madame Maigret, of their apartment in Boulevard Richard-Lenoir, and the brightly lit Grands Boulevards, where he would take her, his very first evening back, to their usual cinema.

When he passed the village hall, sitting in the van's front passenger seat, there was a light in the Gastins' house. In an hour or two, the teacher would return home, and the three of them, so alike one another, would be together again, as if hunkering down on a lost island.

A little later, he did not notice that what were swinging back and forth in the darkness, to his right, were the masts of boats, and at the station he bought a whole heap of Paris newspapers.